The Deadly Game

Lynn Sheft

Cove Press

This book is a work of fiction. Names, characters, places, and incidents are the product of the author's imagination or are used fictitiously. Any resemblance to actual events, locales, or persons, living or dead, is coincidental.

For my parents may they rest in peace. And for Barry, Valerie, Elijah and Judy who support me with their love and good humor.

The future belongs to those who believe in the beauty of their dreams.

--*Eleanor Roosevelt*

Chapter 1

Lauren Casey followed her husband on her bike when he suddenly raced off.

"Michael, wait up," she yelled.

They rode from Bayshore Drive onto the Ingraham Highway's bike path, a shady banyan-lined, two-lane street in Miami's fashionable Coconut Grove district. They left their car parked at Monty's Restaurant after a leisurely lunch overlooking Biscayne Bay. After enjoying conch fritters, Cole Slaw, French fries and an iced tea, racing was the last thing she wanted to do. Their destination was scenic Matheson Hammock Park where a shallow lagoon was refreshed by the tidal action of Biscayne Bay while coconut palms swayed in the breeze.

Lauren focused on down shifting the gears to make it easier to pedal and called after him again, "Michael! Wait!"

When she looked up, Michael was out of sight. Frustrated, she shouted, "Michael, wait for me, will you?" Revving engines and horn blasts of impatient drivers on the street drowned out her words. Determined to catch up to her husband, she sped along the narrow path maneuvering around ficus trees whose gnarled roots broke through the asphalt. She ducked her head to avoid getting hit in the face by a low branch and panted from the exertion. Beads of sweat dotted her forehead and she used the back of her hand to wipe it away.

Is he playing that damn game again? He would take the lead, riding in front of her. Then without warning, he'd race off and duck out of sight behind a tree or down a side street. Once Lauren passed his hiding spot, he'd ride up alongside of her and tap her on the shoulder. The first time he had done it, she screamed, nearly falling off her bike. Yet no matter how many times he played his game, Michael always startled her. The game was wearing thin on Lauren and she would have to speak to him about it.

At the end of busy Ingraham Highway, she turned on Douglas Road in Coral Gables, a residential area of single-family homes where adjacent streets branched off, a convenient place for Michael to duck out of sight. She slowed down expecting him to pop out of his hiding place any minute. The cacophony of the traffic faded as rode on.

Okay Michael, show up. Tap me on the shoulder. I'm ready for you. You can't scare me! Douglas Road ended at Edgewater Drive where apartment buildings and condos fronted Coral Gables Waterway. She turned right and only saw parked cars on the sides of the street. No bicyclists. It was eerily quiet, only the call of seagulls broke the silence. *Could Michael be at the apartment building where I used to live, talking to someone?*

She continued pedaling, hoping for the best as she approached the parking lot of the apartment building. She took another deep breath and swallowed hard. No one was there. Just empty cars heating up as the day wore on. *This is odd. Ingraham Highway is up ahead. He's never gone this far before. If I don't see him, I'll come back and check with Stu. Where are you Michael?*

She recalled living in Stu's apartment building when she was in her twenties and single. Stu, at forty-five, was a divorced man who made a good living from several rental properties in Coconut Grove, Coral Gables and Kendall. Previously, he was a successful wealth manager for a prestigious brokerage firm on Wall Street and retired at forty. His dream was to open a Bed and Breakfast in Vermont with his wife Maureen until the day she served him with divorce papers. He explained to Lauren that Maureen fell in love with their neighbor who lavished attention on her in Stu's absence. With no children to keep him in Manhattan, he fled to South Florida where he spent his leisure hours playing golf at Coral Gables Country Club or taking his boat out for a day of sport fishing. She found him attractive. His green eyes were a startling contrast to his suntanned skin and brown hair. He was genial, but cautious. Lauren never saw him with a woman. He spent his time with golfing or fishing buddies.

Approaching the crest of a small incline, she rose off the saddle. She was approaching Ingraham Highway. *Where are you Michael? This is crazy. How can this be?*

As she rounded the corner, she swallowed back the bile that was creeping up her throat. *Michael, oh Lord!* She looked at her wrist watch and saw that almost twenty minutes had passed since she last saw him. Tears filled her eyes, spilling down her sunburned cheeks and spotting her pink T-shirt. She stopped, unable to go on.

She inhaled sharply. *Get a grip. Call him.* She dug through the saddle bag looking for her cell phone. Not finding it, she cursed. It was in her car. She wiped her eyes and grabbed her water bottle from the holder. She gulped down water, rinsing away the sour taste in her mouth.

Her hopes rose as a twenty-something couple on a tandem bike headed toward her.

"Excuse me," Lauren said, "did you see a young guy wearing a red and black jersey on a bike?"

The man shrugged, "No, sorry." The blond on the back of the bike smiled vacantly.

Lauren got on the saddle and coasted back to the apartment building. The two-story stucco U-shaped building had twelve one- and two-bedroom apartments with the swimming pool and sundeck in the center. She noticed the lounge chairs weren't occupied. *Odd,* she thought. *The skies were clear and football season was long gone. Where is everyone?*

She wheeled her bike to Stu's apartment, a corner unit on the ground floor. She rang the doorbell. *Oh God. What am I going to do?* She was about to leave when she heard the clunk of the deadbolt.

"Lauren, how have you been? It has been ages since I've seen you. What brings you here?" Stu said, opening the door wide and gesturing for her to come in. He wore denim cut-offs, a blue T-shirt and cheap black flip-flops. Lauren entered and paced the floor. Except for the Sunday newspapers spread out on a glass cocktail table, the apartment reflected the touches of an interior decorator with everything in its place. All the colors in the room—from the walls, furniture, throw pillows, and accessories —were coordinated in tones of beige and green. Framed abstract oil paintings hung on the pale sage walls. Potted peace lily, palms and Boston ferns instilled life into the room.

"Stu, have you seen Michael? Did you see him ride by?" Lauren asked, barely getting the words out. She took a deep breath and exhaled with a sigh.

He rubbed his chin. "No, I haven't been outside. It's too damn hot. I've either been on the computer or watching TV.

Ignoring his question, Lauren said, "Stu, I can't find Michael. We were riding our bikes. And then he rode off, playing his stupid game. He's never gone far without coming up behind me and scaring me. I'm worried something happened to him. What if he was hit by a car and he's in a ditch somewhere? You know there's no barrier between the bike path and the street."

Stu walked over to her, taking her elbow. "What are you rambling about? Sit down and tell me what happened."

"I can't sit," Lauren said, shaking his hand off her arm. "We parked our cars at Monty's and had lunch. Then we got on our bikes to ride to the park at Matheson Hammock. Michael raced off. I tried, but I couldn't catch up to him. He disappeared. There's got to be an explanation. Oh, my lord. I'm scared."

"Lauren, you could use a drink. You're trembling." Stu went into the kitchen and opened the liquor cabinet. "Do you want a Scotch and soda?"

"No! Are you crazy? I've got to find Michael!" she shouted.

"I'm sorry, Lauren. You're upset." Reaching for a tall glass and filling it with ice and water, Stu said, "Then just some ice water." He returned to the living room and handed her the glass.

"Did you try calling him?" Stu asked.

"I don't have my cell phone with me. I forgot it in the car," Lauren said, frowning.

"You can use my phone," Stu said handing her his mobile phone.

Lauren looked up, trying to remember Michael's number. She punched in the number and listened until it went to voice mail. "Michael, I'm looking for you. I'm at Stu's apartment. I left my cell phone in the car."

Lauren's brows knitted together. "No answer."

Stu took the phone from Lauren and said, "Lauren, you want to go look for him?"

"Oh yes!" Her mouth felt like cotton and she took long swallows of the water before putting the empty glass down on the table. "And if we don't see him?" she whispered in a quivering voice.

"Then we'll call the police. They'll find him." He grabbed his keys and walked to the door. "Come on. Put your bike in my apartment. You don't want it to get stolen."

What if we don't find Michael? She thought, wheeling the bike into Stu's apartment. *Oh, dear God, please let him be all right.*

"Okay, let's go," Lauren said as she rushed from Stu's poolside apartment to the tree-shaded parking lot.

Chapter 2

The jet black Porsche Boxster was parked in the custom-built carport to protect it from the elements. Stu drove along Edgewater Drive, the distinctive rumble of the engine breaking the silence of the residential street. He braked at the intersection, a tough spot to merge onto Ingraham Highway, a scenic two-lane stretch of road that ran through Coconut Grove, Coral Gables, and South Miami. He waited impatiently, revving the engine while the procession of vans, sports cars, Harleys, and even vintage automobiles drove by.

Lauren peered out the car windows, looking from left to right, hoping for some sign of Michael as Stu drove, following the traffic around Cocoplum Circle and down Sunset Drive. There were men on bikes, but all of them were strangers.

"Stu, I don't think Michael would have gone this far," Lauren said, directing the car's air conditioning vent towards her face. Even though Stu's Porsche had been parked in the shade, it would be several minutes before the AC would cool the stifling interior.

Stu glanced at Lauren. "Did you two have an argument?"

Lauren looked at Stu, raising her eyebrows. "No, why?"

"Well, if he was angry he might have taken off to cool down," Stu offered.

"No! Of course not! How can you suggest such a thing? I have a bad feeling. Please, ride up to Red Road, turn around and go back to your place so I can call the police. I know it. Something's not right. Michael could have been hit by a car and thrown into the bushes. Who would ever see him from the road or even the bike path?" In a voice barely above a whisper Lauren said. "If anything happened to Michael, I don't know what I'll do."

She put her hands over her eyes as her tears fell down her cheeks. Her chest hitched as she tried to catch her breath.

"I'm sorry. I shouldn't have said that. I'm just speaking from personal experience. Lauren, don't cry. Come on. There are some tissues in the glove compartment. Dry your eyes." He patted her hand. "We'll find Michael."

"What if we don't," Lauren whimpered. She didn't want to think about horrible things, but those thoughts of Michael overwhelmed her.

Lauren slouched in the Porsche's tan leather seats. She wiped her face with her hands and saw the black streaks from her mascara. She glanced over at him and inhaled deeply. She pulled out a few tissues from the package to wipe the mascara stains from her cheeks.

She was staring blankly out of the window when Stu finally parked his car in the car port. He got out and went around to open the passenger door for Lauren.

"Come on, Lauren. Let's call the police." He extended his hand to help her out.

Stu unlocked the apartment door and Lauren rushed to the phone and dialed 911.

"How may I direct your call? Police, fire, or medical emergency?" the dispatcher asked.

"Police," Lauren answered, clutching the gold heart that hung from on a chain around her neck.

"Hold on. I'll connect you," the dispatcher said.

Within seconds she was connected to another voice.

"May I help you?" the dispatcher asked.

"My husband has disappeared. I think something awful has happened to him," Lauren said as she dabbed her eyes with the crumpled tissue.

"What's your name, Mrs. ...?"

"Lauren Casey."

"Where are you now?" the dispatcher asked.

"At twenty-two Edgewater Drive, Coral Gables. Apartment six on the ground floor.

"All right, Mrs. Casey. I'll send an officer out right now to take a report." The dispatcher repeated the address.

"Okay," Lauren sighed and hung up the receiver. "Oh, dear God, do you think they can find him, Stu?"

"I hope so, Lauren. Sit down. Someone should be here soon."

"This whole thing doesn't make sense. How could he simply disappear? This is a nightmare." She looked at her watch and sat on the edge of the couch. "My lord, it's been at least an hour. An ordinary Sunday bike ride and then..." Lauren broke down in tears.

The room was quiet except for the sound of Lauren sniffling. Finally Stu said, "I wish I could make things better. I can't imagine what could have happened to him. He was an avid bike rider. Did you tell me he could go the distance? Entered races?"

"Yes."

There was a knock at the door and Stu put down his glass of water on the cocktail table to answer it. Lauren sprung up from the couch. A uniformed officer was at the threshold. A name tag over his breast pocket identified him as Chandler.

"Is Lauren Casey here?" Chandler asked. He towered over Stu, had brown hair that had a hint of gray at the temples, and blue eyes.

Lauren cleared her throat and said, "I'm Lauren."

Stepping into the apartment, the policeman said, "I'm Officer Chandler. Tell me what happened."

After Lauren composed herself, she told the officer all the details leading up to Michael's disappearance and the fruitless search that Stu and she had made.

"You understand that adults are allowed to be missing, don't you Mrs. Casey?" asked Chandler. "That's why we usually don't act on a disappearance for twenty-four hours."

"But he could be hurt," Lauren sniffed "I need to find him."

"I understand your anguish. That's why I'm here." In a gentler tone of voice, Chandler asked, "Has this ever happened before, Mrs. Casey?"

"What do you mean?"

"I mean, has your husband gone away before without an explanation?"

"No, never." Lauren could feel the jackhammer in her chest.

"Was he taking any medications?"

"Just an antihistamine for allergies."

"Has he been under stress lately?"

"No more than the usual."

"What do you mean by that?"

"I mean, Michael is in sales and he has quotas to meet. He always wants to surpass them."

"I see. You said you were bike riding."

"Yes, we go every weekend, if the weather's nice."

"Do you live in this building?"

Lauren shook her head no. "I used to live here before we got married."

"I'll need your home address and phone number as well as an alternate number if you have one."

Lauren dictated the information as the officer filled in the report.

"Can you give me a physical description?"

"He has short brown hair, brown eyes, thirty-seven years-old, weight I'd guess to be one-seventy, height, I think five-eight."

"Would you happen to have a recent picture of him?"

"Yes, let me get it," Lauren said, walking to her bicycle. She unzipped the saddle bag and pulled out her small wallet. She handed a photo of Michael to the officer.

"Thank you." Chandler looked at the photo and slipped it into his breast pocket. "I'll file this report and I'll also enter this information into the government database."

"Is that like a 'be on the lookout?'" Lauren asked full of hope.

"No, we would in cases of older people who might suffer from dementia or with young children. I'm sorry to say, Mrs. Casey, no missing report is filed on an adult for twenty-four hours."

"Then what's the point of putting the information in the computer?"

"Well, if an officer detains someone for some reason, like a traffic violation, we can get their name and date of birth and see what comes up."

"I find this frustrating that you won't look for my husband for twenty-four hours," Lauren said.

"I'm sorry, Mrs. Casey. Do you need a way to get home?"

"I'll take you, Lauren," Stu volunteered.

Chandler looked at Lauren for her reaction. Lauren nodded that she accepted Stu's offer.

"All right, then. I'll be on my way," Chandler said. Stu followed the officer, closing the door behind him. Lauren stared at the door, frozen in her exasperation.

"Do you want me to take you to your car and come back here to get your bike now?" Stu asked.

"I can't believe they're not doing anything about this," Lauren said ignoring Stu's question.

"Lauren, did you hear me?"

"No, what?"

"Do you want me to take you to your car or what?"

"Yes, please," Lauren said. She put her hands to her forehead and closed her eyes. Then she abruptly dropped her hands to her sides.

"Are you sure you'll be able to drive?"

"I'll be all right."

"Do you want to hang out here awhile longer? Have a drink or something?"

"No, I better get going. Maybe Michael will try to call me at home since I forgot my cell phone. Maybe he left me a message on both phones."

Both Stu and Lauren remained silent during the ride to Monty's. Lauren replayed the scene in her mind again starting from the time she was changing gears on her bike. She tried to find answers to his disappearance. *How could Michael just vanish like that? If he did get hit by a car and was thrown in the underbrush, he's either dead or unconscious. And if he's unconscious, who knows how long he'll be out. A brain injury! I can't think about it! And if he comes to, maybe he'll get help. Maybe someone found him and called an ambulance. I'm sure Michael has his wallet in the bike bag. Then someone will call me at home. Maybe they already have. Oh, God, let him be alive! Oh, Michael! Where are you? Please, dear Lord, let me hear from him. I don't know what I'd do without you, Michael. Why did I even fiddle with the stupid gears? I should have kept going and not let him out of my sight! And now? I don't know what to think.*

"Lauren, we're here," Stu said, breaking Lauren out of her brooding.

"Wait until I check my phone before you leave." She got out and rushed to her car. Yanking the door open, she found her phone laying on the seat. It was warm to the touch as the car was super-heated. She looked at the screen and saw there were no new phone calls. *I have to get home as soon as I can. Wouldn't it be wonderful if he were waiting for me at home? Ridiculous. He would have left a message on your cell.*

She shook her head at Stu. "No messages. I'll meet you back at your place to get my bike." She started the car and put the air conditioning on full blast, adjusting the vents to her face.

Stu waved to her. "Lauren, be careful. Keep your mind on driving."

Once they arrived at the apartment building, Stu retrieved Lauren's bike and mounted it on the car's bike rack.

Stu approached Lauren's open car window. "Lauren, do you still have my phone number?"

"I think I do." Lauren checked her contacts list in her phone. "Yes, here it is."

"Good. Call me if you hear something? Or just to talk. Promise?"

"Sure, Stu. Thanks for driving around."

As she turned the ignition, the distinctive thump, thump, thump of a helicopter overhead caught their attention.

"Don't worry, Lauren, they'll start looking for him soon," said Stu, glancing up at the clear blue sky.

Lauren nodded with resignation, backed the car out of the parking space, and drove away. She glanced at her cell phone on the console wishing it would ring. She called Michael and left another message. On the way home, she passed several patrol cars and hoped their mission was to find her husband. By the time she pulled into her driveway and engaged the automatic garage door opener, it was twilight. There were a few school-age children playing street hockey in the quiet neighborhood of single-family homes. She parked her car in the garage next to Michael's compact car. Seeing his car made her heart leap. *Where was he?* She returned her bike to its place against the side wall. After closing the garage door and disabling the house alarm, she rushed to turn on the lamp in the family room. She went directly to her office. The message light was blinking on her answering machine and the display panel indicated there was one message. Hoping it was Michael, she played the recorded message.

"Lauren, it's Judy. Give me a call when you get a minute. It's nothing important."

Lauren erased the message and stared blankly at the phone. Easing herself into the black leather chair at her desk, she picked up the phone and dialed her best friend's number.

"Hello."

"Judy, it's me, Lauren."

"What's the matter? You sound awful. Are you sick?"

"You could say that. Michael's missing."

"What?" Judy yelled.

"Michael's missing."

"I don't understand. How can he be missing?"

"We went for a bike ride through the Grove like we usually do on Sunday and he rode off and then vanished. I stopped at the apartment building where I used to live. Stu and I drove around looking for him. We didn't find him," Lauren said, breaking down in tears.

"How could he just disappear? It doesn't make sense," Judy said.

Barely able to get the words out through her sobs, Lauren said, "I don't know. The only thing I can think of is that maybe he got hit by a car and was thrown into the bushes."

"But wouldn't the driver stop?"

"You would think. But some of these people…"

"Have you called the police?"

"Yes, from Stu's place, but nothing's being done."

"What do you mean? Nothing's being done?"

"The officer took a report. He said adults are allowed to be missing. They won't do anything for twenty-four hours."

"Oh, Lauren, I'm so sorry. You must be scared out of your mind. Do you want me to come over?"

"I don't want to interfere with your plans."

"Don't be silly. No plans. You know, work the next morning. You shouldn't be alone. I'll be right over."

"All right. Thanks, Judy. Be careful driving over."

With tears streaming down her face, Lauren called Michael's cell phone. When he didn't answer, she left another message for him to call her at home. Then she went into the kitchen and poured herself a drink. She felt lost and went through the house mechanically, closing the wood blinds in each bedroom while dabbing her eyes with another tissue. When she returned to the family room, she turned on the TV to the evening news. She sat down on the couch, sipping her drink. The alcohol sedated her and she stopped crying. She tried to concentrate on what the news anchors were saying but she was distracted. Her mind replayed the events of the afternoon and settled on an image of Michael lying in a jungle of twisted vines and thorny bushes. She shook her head like a wet dog to rid her brain of the gory image.

She looked up the phone numbers for the local hospitals from her cell phone. There were four that she remembered. The results were the same. No man fitting Michael's description or name had been admitted to their facility. She didn't want to think the worst, but the thought of Michael dead pushed into her mind and she became hysterical. The tears flowed and her body shuddered as she sobbed. She cried out, "Oh, please dear God, please let Michael be all right. Oh, God, please, please, please."

She was torn between the idea of searching for him again or of staying home in case he came home. She paced the floor and then stopped in front of the oak wall unit that flanked one wall. Among the books, art objects and framed photos, she focused on their wedding picture. Her mind flashed to that wonderful day when she felt like a princess next to her handsome groom.

The doorbell rang, jarring her from her thoughts. She walked to the front door, wiping her eyes. Looking through the peephole, she saw Judy. A breeze tousled her short red hair and she raked her fingers through it to smooth it back into place. Standing five-seven, Judy had a full figure that she kept under control by working out at the gym. Lauren opened the door and sighed with relief.

"Oh, Lauren. You look awful. Come on. Let's sit down. Do you want a drink? Oh, you already have one. Mind if I have one, too?" Judy said, putting her arm around the shoulder of her friend and guiding her to the family room. She wore her weekend uniform of distressed jeans, tank top, and Birkenstock sandals. A sparkling diamond solitaire pendant hung from a gold chain around her neck. Judy had reset the gem from her engagement ring after her divorce.

"Go right ahead, help yourself," Lauren said settling back down at her place on the couch. "Do you mind giving me a refill on this one?"

"Sure," Judy said, taking Lauren's glass and sniffing it. "Do you have any Seagram's? I hate Scotch."

"Yes, there's Seagram's in the lower kitchen cabinet on the right side of the refrigerator."

Judy made the drinks and took them into the family room. Lauren had quieted from crying, but her eyes glistened and were red-rimmed. Her hand trembled as she lifted the drink to her mouth.

"You must be out of your mind with worry," Judy said after she took a sip of her Seagram's and soda.

"Oh, Lord," said Lauren. "I feel so helpless. Here I am, just sitting here. I feel like I should go look for him again."

"I don't think that a good idea. Leave it to the police to find him," Judy said, sitting down at the other end of the couch.

Lauren put her drink down on the glass-top table in front of her and cupped her hands together in prayer. "I just hope he's alive."

The doorbell rang, startling both women. Lauren looked at Judy, who had a look of concern in her brown eyes.

"I think you better answer that," Judy said. "It could be the police."

Lauren got up from her seat, took a deep breath, exhaled, and walked to the door. Looking through the peephole, she saw a man standing outside wearing a white dress shirt and skinny tie. He was tall, about six-foot-two Lauren guessed, with blonde hair and a mustache.

"Who is it?" Lauren asked through the door.

"I'm Detective Dolan with Miami-Dade Police," the man said, offering his identification.

Lauren opened the door.

"Are you Mrs. Michael Casey?"

"Yes, what is it? Have you found my husband?"

"May I come in and talk to you?" the detective asked.

Lauren felt her stomach lurch to her throat and she swallowed hard. "Of course. Come in, detective."

"Why don't you sit down," Detective Dolan suggested.

Lauren led the way to the family room.

"This is my friend, Judy Miller." Lauren sat down on the couch and gestured to the love seat as a place for the detective to sit. He remained standing.

"Mrs. Casey, I'm afraid I have bad news. I just came from the scene. A resident in the Grove was leaving to go to dinner when he found your husband's body on his front lawn."

Chapter 3

When Lauren opened her eyes, she saw Judy and Detective Dolan standing over her. She was lying on the couch with a throw pillow under her head. "Lauren, you fainted," Judy said. "I'm so sorry about Michael."

Lauren sat up, slowly realizing that Michael's death was not just a bad dream but reality. She stared blankly, rubbing her temples and her forehead. She shook her head, trying to concentrate. Shivering, she reached for the blanket that was slung over the arm of the couch and put it around her shoulders. After a moment, she mumbled, "He's dead? He was hit by a car?"

"No. I'm afraid not. It's a homicide. He was shot in the head," Detective Dolan answered.

"Shot? Oh my God! That can't be! Are you sure?" The horror of what she had just heard flashed a mental picture and Lauren sobbed.

The detective nodded.

"Where did you find him?" Lauren struggled to get the words out.

"In front of a home on a side street, off Douglas Road on East Sunrise. When the owner was leaving for dinner, he discovered your husband's body and his bike. Fortunately, your husband carried identification in his saddlebag. Do you know the street?" asked Detective Dolan.

"Not really. I didn't go down any of those side streets to look for him. I guess I should have. He might be alive right now."

Judy and Detective Dolan looked at each other. Judy sat down next to Lauren, draping her arm around her friend's shoulder. "Lauren, I don't understand. Who would have this? Why?"

"Mrs. Casey, you said 'to look for him.' I saw in our database that you reported him missing," Detective Dolan said before Lauren had a chance to answer Judy.

"That's right. I reported him missing some hours ago," Lauren said. "Can I see him?"

"Yes, Mrs. Casey, but first, in order to find out who killed your husband, I'm going to ask you strictly routine questions. Do you own a gun?" asked Detective Dolan.

"No, of course not," said Lauren, shaking her head. She glanced at Judy whose eyes were wide with fear.

The detective continued to probe. "Did Michael own a gun?"

"No, he talked about buying one, but I said no. I'm afraid of guns. I didn't want one in the house."

"Mrs. Casey, was your husband employed?"

"Yes," Lauren answered. "He's a pharmaceutical salesman. He calls on doctors presenting the company's prescription drugs."

"What's the name of the company?" Detective Dolan asked, taking notes.

"Goldsmith & Kline, they're out by the airport."

"How long did he work there?"

"Just about two years."

"Who were his close friends?"

Lauren leaned forward, and with a shaking hand, took a sip from her drink. "Just me. He had close friends in high school and college. He hung out with some work friends before we were married, but not now. Sure he'd go to lunch with people, but not meet anyone after work. I can't imagine who would have killed him."

"Did he ever talk about anyone at work who may have had a grudge? Another salesman, perhaps?"

"I don't think so. Michael never mentioned it."

"Did your husband gamble?"

"Not really. Just the Florida lottery if you call that gambling.

"How long have you been married?"

"Six months," Lauren said, glancing over at their wedding portrait on the shelf. Lauren stood up, tears welling up in her eyes. "Will you excuse me a minute?"

Lauren walked into the bathroom and closed the door. She looked at herself in the mirror and took a deep breath. She wiped her tears with a tissue, and took a drink of water. She tried to stop crying, but a deep ache in her chest forced her to let her grief spill out. She couldn't believe what the detective had told her -- Michael was dead. Surely there had to be some mistake. When she had no more tears, she soaked a wash cloth with cold water from the sink and held it over her swollen eyelids. The coolness felt soothing to her hot skin. Finally, she opened the bathroom door.

Returning to the family room, she didn't know how much longer she could endure the questioning. She wanted everyone to go away and have Michael home. She caught the tail end of Judy responding to Detective Dolan, "...we work together at an ad agency in Miami." Lauren took her place back on the couch next to Judy. She looked at Detective Dolan and nodded for him to continue.

"Do you have any children?"

"No, we've only been married six months." Lauren looked at the detective, raising her eyebrows.

"I was thinking from a previous marriage," Detective Dolan offered.

"This is the first marriage for both Michael and me."

"I'm sorry to have to ask you this, but do you know if your husband was seeing another woman. Could there have been an old girlfriend that he's seen lately?"

"No. Michael and I dated each other for five years before we got married. He wasn't seeing anyone. I don't know when he'd have the time. He goes to work and comes home right afterward. We spend our evenings and weekends together. No, I don't think there was another woman." Lauren let out a deep sigh. "Detective, I'm wiped out. I can't think straight."

Detective Dolan glanced at his watch. "I understand. And I'm sorry. But just another minute, please. Did Michael take any trips out of the area recently?"

Lauren shook her head no.

"Did he have any hobbies, like fishing?"

"No, we don't own a boat," said Lauren.

"What did he do when he wasn't working?"

"He likes to ride his bike, read. I don't know, we spend a lot of time together, going to dinner, movies, concerts, that sort of thing." Lauren looked at her watch. "You know, I probably better make some phone calls -- his parents -- mine."

"All right, Mrs. Casey," Detective Dolan said, "I know this a terrible shock to you. But I'd like you to make a formal statement at headquarters in a few days. We don't have to do it right away. How about Wednesday or Thursday?

"Oh, I don't know. I guess Thursday will be fine," Lauren agreed.

"And I'd like you to take a polygraph test. It's strictly voluntary, of course."

"A polygraph? What for?" Lauren asked, walking the detective to the door.

"I'm sure you don't mind. It's just procedure. We'll be questioning a lot of people, those that he came in contact with. People who know the both of you. We've questioned some of the residents on East Sunrise where he was found."

"Did anybody see anything?" Lauren asked. "Or hear anything?"

"Apparently not."

"You said I can see him," Lauren stammered. "Michael."

Detective Dolan nodded, "Yes. You can see him at the morgue. You can identify the body. If you change your mind about seeing him, identification can be made with dental records. You know in cases of homicide there will be an autopsy."

The detective took the business card holder from his pocket and struggled to pull a single card from the pack and offered it to Lauren. "Feel free to call me."

"Thank you," Lauren said taking the card from him. Lauren opened the door and the detective walked out to his car. The wind had picked up and Lauren looked up at the storm clouds overhead. Dead leaves from the black olive trees blew across the street and settled along the curb. The fronds of the Queen Anne palm tree rustled in the breeze.

"Looks like we might get some rain tonight," Detective Dolan observed. He started to get in his car, hesitated and said, "I'm sorry for your loss, Mrs. Casey. I want to solve this crime as much as you do."

Lauren nodded, took a deep breath, and closed the door. She turned around and looked at Judy who rushed to her and hugged her tightly. The two stood there silently, soaking each other's shoulders with their tears. After what seemed like a long time, the two friends separated and wiped their own eyes with their fingers. They looked at each other and saw each other's pain. Judy pulled tissues out of her jeans pocket, wiped her eyes and handed a clean one to Lauren.

"What do I do now?" Lauren cried. "What do I do now? I can't believe he's dead. I just can't believe it. We just went for a bike ride. And now he's dead. It doesn't make any sense. Who would have done this? Who would kill Michael? It's insane!"

Judy let out a long sigh and said, "I'm really sorry, Lauren. And I can't believe it, either. It seems incredible. Why Michael? He's the nicest guy. Everybody who meets him thinks he's great. He always had a smile on his face. And he's so nice. He was always ready to help you with anything. Remember when the shelving collapsed in my pantry? You mentioned it to him and he insisted on reinstalling it for me. I don't understand. Who would have killed him? And why? He's a straight arrow guy."

The two friends sat down in silence and then Judy said, "You'll have to let his parents know and yours what happened. Are you up to it?"

"No," Lauren admitted, picking up her glass from the table and carrying it into the kitchen. She made herself another drink, a double this time. "But I'll have to." She stood there staring at her glass.

"You better have dinner if you're drinking," Judy said.

"I know. And I haven't offered you anything to eat. Are you hungry?"

"You know me. I can always eat, especially when I'm upset. Do you have anything in the fridge or can I get something delivered?"

Judy sat down at the kitchen table and watched Lauren look through the refrigerator and freezer. She closed the doors to both compartments and turned around to face Judy. "I don't know. I can't think. My mind is blank. Just order something for yourself, okay?"

Lauren took a seat opposite Judy, put her elbows on the table and rested her forehead in the palms of her hands.

Judy pulled her smart phone from her pocket. "Will you eat pizza?"

"I don't know. I'm not hungry. Just order it," Lauren said. She wondered how she was going to tell Mom Casey about Michael. She still couldn't comprehend that she'd never see her husband alive. Just a few hours ago she was with Michael. Now he's dead.

"Okay." Judy searched through the listings on her phone found the number for Pappy's Pizza and placed the order. "It'll be twenty to thirty minutes." She sat down at the table.

"Where's your drink?" Lauren scanned the kitchen counters.

"I left it in the other room. I'll get it." Judy got up and retrieved her drink. "Lauren, come sit here. It's more comfortable here on the couch."

"I should make those calls." Lauren picked up the house phone and called her parents. She let the phone ring a dozen times before hanging up.

"They must be out to dinner. I'll try calling Mom Casey." Lauren paced the floor waiting for someone to answer her call. She wondered how she would break the news to her mother-in-law. She played with the gold locket at her neck.

Ending the connection, Lauren said, "No luck at their house, either. Guess they're out to dinner, too. They don't have an answering machine or a cell phone. I'll try them later."

Lauren sat down on the couch and swallowed her drink. "I can't believe someone killed Michael. Why? Why would someone do such a thing?"

"I don't know. Maybe he was mixed up with some people he didn't tell you about," Judy suggested.

"Like what kind of people?"

"I don't know. Maybe he witnessed something he shouldn't have, like a drug deal or something."

"I think if he did, Michael would have told me," Lauren said thinking that Michael was always open with her.

"I mean at the time he was killed. Maybe he was at the wrong place at the wrong time," said Judy. "Maybe he witnessed something."

They both sat there silently in their own thoughts for a long time. Lauren tried to remember names of people Michael had mentioned in the past. She tried to come up with a reason why someone would kill him. Reviewing their lives, she was stumped for an answer. She wondered if there was something he had kept from her. Some dark secret perhaps? Was he living another life she didn't know about?

Outside, the rain came in drops and then the sky opened up in a downpour. There was the sound of thunder and a few seconds later, the crack of lightning. The doorbell rang, startling both of them. Lauren got her wallet, checked to see if it was the pizza delivery, and answered the door.

"That will be fourteen eight-nine," the delivery boy said, sliding the cardboard pizza box out of its red vinyl insulated carrier and handing it to her. Lauren looked at him, thinking he looked awfully young to be driving. She took the box from him and handed him a twenty dollar bill. "Here, keep it."

The boy thanked her and ran through the rain to his battered car.

"Great, I'm starved," Judy said, going into the kitchen to get plates and napkins.

Lauren set the box down on the glass-top coffee table in front of the couch. "Do you want something else to drink with the pizza?"

"A glass of water would be nice."

"Okay," Lauren said walking into the kitchen. She took a glass from the cabinet and filled it with cold water from the refrigerator dispenser. She placed it on the table in front of Judy. "Go ahead and help yourself to pizza."

Judy opened the box and pulled a slice away from the rest of the pie, the strings of white cheese dripping down. "Mm, good, " Judy said after taking a bite. Lauren stared silently at the pizza. "Aren't you having some?"

Lauren looked at Judy and sighed. "I really don't feel like eating."

"Try to eat something. You've been drinking on an empty stomach. So come on. *Mange, mange.*"

Lauren took a slice of pizza with the onion topping and took a bite. She chewed it deliberately as if she had never eaten pizza before in her life. She dropped the slice on the plate and took a deep breath. She had no appetite. Maybe she could eat later.

"Do you want me to tell Greg in the morning about Michael or will you call him?" Judy asked. Greg was a partner and creative director of the advertising agency where they both worked, Judy as a senior art director and Lauren as a senior copywriter. As their supervisor, Greg took a hands-off approach, letting the two women work together to develop award-wining ad campaigns for some of the agency's biggest clients.

"I think it best if I call him. I know he'll give me as much time off as I need," Lauren said. "If he needs to, he can call in a freelancer on a day-rate basis to fill in for me. Although there's that script I need to finish for the video presentation."

"Lauren, you have enough to deal with right now. Greg can write it himself. After all, he's a copywriter, too," Judy said.

"I suppose so," Lauren said getting up from the couch and heading to the kitchen, "I'm going to try calling Mom Casey again."

Lauren picked up the phone and placed the call to Michael's parents. She took a deep breath and slowly exhaled. On the third ring, Michael's mother picked up. "Hello."

"Mom Casey, it's Lauren. I tried calling you earlier."

"Lauren, darling. It's good to hear your voice. We just got back from dinner with the Russells," Mom Casey explained.

"Mom Casey, I'm afraid I have bad news."

Chapter 4

Lauren lay on the king-size bed with the sheet up to her chest. Groggy with sleep, she barely opened one eye and saw a striped pattern of sunlight on the bedroom wall cast by the partially open blinds. The storm had passed and it was already eighty-five degrees outside. She turned on her side and draped her right arm on Michael's side of the bed. When it landed with a thud on the mattress, Lauren was thrown back into reality. She sat up in bed and looked at the empty space next to her, remembering the horrible night.

After she gave the terrible news to Mom Casey, Michael's father, Eddie, got on the phone. She could hear Mom Casey crying in the background. He, too, was overwhelmed with grief. When Lauren raised the question about the site for the funeral and burial, they agreed to have it in Miami. Eddie said one of them would call Lauren on Monday once their airline reservations were made. Lauren invited them to stay at her house, but they declined, opting to stay at a nearby hotel. It was just as well since Lauren's parents would be staying at her house. After hanging up with her in-laws, Lauren called her parents. Again, the brutal, numbing shock. Her mother told her they would fly down and stay with her for as long as they were needed. They, too, would try to get reservations for Monday.

Lauren looked at the clock radio on the oak nightstand. The digital display was seven-zero-five. She didn't remember what time she finally went to bed, but she knew it was midnight when she said good night to Judy. Her friend offered to spend the night, but Lauren insisted that Judy go home so she could get a good night's sleep in her own bed.

They had spent the evening talking about Michael. Lauren reminisced about the first time she had met him.

That was five years ago. There was no "significant other" in her life as Lauren had just gotten over a two-year love affair with a man who had more problems than Lauren could handle. She dated casually, but the men meant nothing more than having someone with which to spend a few hours. At twenty-five years old, she was ready for a relationship, but she wanted to be certain it was with a man who was right for her, one who shared common goals and dreams. She decided to make a list of the attributes that she believed most important in a mate. In doing so, she realized how much she had matured since her college days. No longer was being handsome number one on her list. Instead, the first thing Lauren wrote was "intelligent," then "honest," "considerate," "thoughtful," " sense of humor," "hard worker." The list went on and on. Reference to appearance was "good-looking" and it was much further down on the list. She remembered she had made the list on a Monday and put it in her drawer. By Friday, Lauren had plans for the weekend. She had a dinner date Friday night at eight with Jeff. Saturday she planned to go out to a movie with another man whose name she now could no longer remember. Then Friday afternoon a media buyer at work invited her to attend a birthday party for a radio station sales rep. It was scheduled for six o'clock at a popular restaurant and lounge in Coconut Grove. Lauren accepted, figuring she could spend an hour or so before she had to be at her apartment where her date would pick her up. With a laugh, she said, "Sure, you never know. I just might meet Prince Charming."

The media buyer, a single woman who had just turned thirty, said, "Yes, you and me both."

The party was held in the private room at Sausalito's, a restaurant and lounge that was the current "in" place to be. The guests had their own cocktail lounge to themselves and it wasn't too long before Lauren was bored with media types talking about points and market share.

"Noreen, I'm leaving. Thank you for inviting me."

"You're leaving already? Are you sure you won't stay for another drink?" Noreen asked watching Lauren set her glass down on the bar.

"No, thanks." On her way out through the main bar, Lauren hesitated. Although bored with the media people, she really didn't feel like going home and debated if she should sit at the main bar and order another drink. She looked at the strangers sitting on bar stools, hoping to see a familiar face. Seeing none, she faltered. She felt conspicuous being unescorted in a bar. Just as she was on her way to the door, Michael came up to her and said, "Hi, my name is Michael Casey. May I buy you a drink?"

Lauren stopped and looked at his warm smile and sincere brown eyes. She thought him handsome and impeccably dressed.

"I'm ready to leave. I was at a private birthday party back there for a media rep and talk of market share and demographics was more than I can stand."

"I promise not to bore you. Believe me, I don't know the difference between a CPM and a RPM."

Laughing, Lauren said, "In that case, I accept. My name is Lauren."

"Do you have a last name, Lauren?"

"Lauren Bacall." Seeing the expression on his face, Lauren burst out laughing.

Rather than sit at the bar, Michael got them a booth where they could converse with some privacy. Lauren couldn't believe how easy it was to talk to him. He was knowledgeable about world and government affairs and had her laughing with his quips. After an hour, she felt as though she had known him for years. He then asked her to join him for dinner. And that's when she remembered she had a date. She looked at her watch. It was already seven-thirty, and she explained she already had a date for dinner so she had to leave immediately. Michael then asked her for Saturday night. Again she declined with the same reason. She hoped he wouldn't give up, thinking she wasn't interested. As she got up from the table he asked her if she minded if he called her sometime. She was relieved. She gave him her business card and asked him to call her at work. She thanked him for the drink, excused herself, and went home to wait for Jeff. She went out on her weekend dates, but her thoughts were of Michael. She hoped he wouldn't let days pass before calling and her prayers were answered Monday afternoon. He invited her out for dinner Saturday. She accepted. They continued to talk and then Michael interrupted her. "Do we have to wait until Saturday night to get together? Can I take you out to dinner tonight?"

"Sure, I'd love to," Lauren answered. His eagerness flattered her.

Lauren remembered the evening. He had picked one of the finest restaurants in Coral Gables and the dinner was excellent. She noticed he focused on her rather than looking at the other women in the room. When they left the restaurant at nine, Michael noticed an old Latina on the corner of the street selling long-stemmed roses and he bought her one. The next day, he called her at work to thank her for a great evening and asked her if he could call her at work or at her apartment before their date Saturday. "Sure," she said giving him her land line and mobile phone numbers. "Any time."

Soon she was getting calls from him twice a day, at work and at home. The rest of the story, as Lauren told Judy, was history. By the second week after meeting each other, they went out every Wednesday and Saturday, and after a few months, they were seeing each other every night and all day Sunday. It was a fabulous beginning and a fabulous romance. She had wonderful memories and she enjoyed reliving them with Judy.

Lauren pushed back the sheet and got out of bed. It was Monday and in a few hours, she knew she'd be on the phone again, delivering bad news and making funeral arrangements.

She went into the master bathroom and switched on the light. Leaning over the marble vanity, she looked at herself in the mirror and thought, *I'm all alone now.*

Emptiness overcame her and she sobbed. She crumbled to the cold tile floor and cried until she had no tears left. She wondered if she was on the verge of a nervous breakdown.

Grabbing the edge of the vanity, she pulled herself up and turned on the shower. She stripped off her aqua nightgown and stepped into the glass-enclosed shower. She put her face directly under the shower head, hoping the water would wash away her grief. She knew she was going to have to pull herself together, especially in front of Mom and Dad Casey. How she would do it, she didn't know.

When she turned off the water, she heard the phone ringing. Isn't that always the way, she thought. Get in the shower and someone will call.

Quickly wrapping her head in a towel, she grabbed another towel off the rack and wrapped it around her body. She darted across the room to the phone on the nightstand.

"Hello."

"Lauren, it's your Mom. You sound like you have a cold."

"No, Mom, I've been crying."

"Of course. I'm sorry, Lauren. I know this is very difficult for you. I'll be there soon. I have the flight information. We'll be flying from Newark Airport on Delta flight..."

Lauren interrupted, "Wait a minute, Mom. Let me get something to write this down."

"Go right ahead."

Lauren pulled open the nightstand drawer and found a notepad and pen. "All right, tell me. That's Delta out of Newark." Lauren wrote down the flight number and arrival time.

"Call before you head out to the airport. You never know if there will be a delay."

"Okay, Mom."

"Oh, Lauren, my baby. This is so horrible. Do you want me to bring you anything?"

"No, Mom, just yourself and Dad. I'll be glad when you're here. I feel lost. It feels so weird in the house without Michael. I can't believe he's gone. I keep expecting to see him."

There was a long pause. Lauren didn't know what else to say. "Well, I got to go, Mom. I just got out of the shower."

"All right, I won't keep you. I'll see you this afternoon. Goodbye, Lauren, and I love you."

"Bye, Mom. I love you, too," Lauren said hanging up the phone.

Lauren dressed, thinking about her mother, Betty. She was a petite woman, only five feet tall and weighed 105 pounds. Her mother had a flair for fashion, having managed a woman's boutique for twenty years. She frequently entertained in her home and when she went to visit, she never went empty handed. She called the presents "hostess gifts" and these tokens were always appreciated by Betty's friends. Lauren looked forward to seeing her mother. More than ever, she needed her mother to tell her everything would be all right, just like when she was a little girl.

Lauren went to the kitchen to make coffee. She drank grapefruit juice and then glanced at her watch and saw that it was almost eight. She decided to wait another hour before calling Michael's office and Greg. She wondered if the newspaper would have a story about Michael. She went out and picked up the plastic-bagged newspaper from the swale which was still wet from the night's downpour.

She returned to the house, peeling off the soggy wrapper. With her coffee in hand, she sat at the table to read the paper.

The telephone rang. By the second ring, Lauren had picked up the receiver.

"Hello."

"Lauren, it's Mom Casey. How are you holding up this morning?"

"Okay. How about you?"

"About the same -- which means we're both lying. Do you have a paper and pencil handy? I'll give you our flight information."

Lauren reached for a pencil and wrote as 38 spoke. She repeated the information to make sure she got it right, then said, "Good. My parents come in at three-fifty so we'll wait for your arrival and come home together."

"Great. I spoke to Michael's brother last night. He and Julie will fly down tomorrow. They're going to call the rest of the family for me this morning since I'm just not thinking straight. I don't know how many will make the trip to Miami. When do think you'll have the funeral?" asked Mom Casey, her voice filled with emotion.

"It depends on when the autopsy is done. But I'm hoping it could be Wednesday or Thursday. Then again it could take longer. I'll be calling the funeral home today. They might be able to give me an idea." Lauren closed her eyes and took a deep breath. She let out a sigh.

"My thoughts exactly, Lauren. I need to lie down. Goodbye."

Lauren went back to the table and sat down, overcome with guilt. She wondered if Mom Casey blamed her for Michael's death. Somehow she felt responsible. If she had kept up with him during the bike ride, he never would have been off by himself.

She sipped the coffee and stared at the newspaper not seeing the words. Anxious, she looked forward to the distraction of calling people and taking care of the arrangements. She turned the pages of the paper, looking for a story about Michael. There was none. Finally, it was nine o'clock. She called Michael's office and spoke to Bob Tiber, the sales director. He was shocked by the news and told her that Michael had made top salesman for January. He asked her about the funeral and she told him she'd be sure to let him know the details once the arrangements were made. She felt oddly detached talking about Michael. It was if she were talking about a casual acquaintance, not her husband.

Lauren then called her office and asked for Greg. The receptionist put the call through.

"Hi, Lauren," Greg Sindelar said cheerfully. "I hope you're not sick."

"Greg, it's much worse than that," Lauren paused, clutching the phone tightly. "Michael's been murdered."

"Murdered! I don't believe it. How? Why? Lauren, tell me," Greg demanded. Lauren told him what she knew, her voice quivering.

"So what are the police going to do about it?" Greg asked.

"They'll be doing an investigation. Plus there's the autopsy. And they want me to take a polygraph test."

"Don't tell me they suspect you?"

"You've seen enough movies to know that they always suspect the spouse until they have reason not to," Lauren said. "But I have nothing to worry about."

"Do you know when you'll have the funeral?" Greg asked.

"Not yet, I'm hoping Wednesday. I hope to know something today," Lauren said, thinking she should call Detective Dolan, "I'll be sure to let you know. My parents and my in-laws are flying in this afternoon."

"Are they all staying with you?"

"Just my folks. The Caseys are staying at a hotel. Of course, they'll be spending most of their time here at my house."

"Well, Lauren," Greg said inhaling sharply, "if there's anything I can do, let me know. Don't worry about the office. What I can't handle, I'll call in Jim Lawrence to free-lance. The only outstanding project is that script to write for the Mirabella video presentation. If you can come back in next week you should have enough time to get it done. But take it easy. Don't worry if you're not able to." Greg was quiet a moment. "I just can't believe this has happened. Michael. Geez, man. I'm truly sorry, Lauren."

"I know, Greg," Lauren said, her voice breaking. "I'll call you back when I know something more."

"Okay. Lauren, speak to you soon. Don't worry about the office and take care."

Lauren ended the call. She went into the family room, found the detective's business card, and returned to the phone. She looked at the card, hesitant to make the call. When she called his number at the Miami-Dade Police Department she was surprised when he answered her call thinking it would go to voice mail.

"Detective Dolan. It's Lauren Casey."

"Yes, Mrs. Casey," Detective Dolan said.

"My family wants to know when we can have a funeral. Do you know when an autopsy will be done?"

"It all depends on how busy the M.E.'s department is."

"Do you think you could find out for me?"

"More than likely someone will be contacting you this morning from the medical examiner's office to come down and identify the body. They can give you an idea when they'll release the body."

"Oh, I see."

"How about if I transfer you to a polygraph examiner so you can make an appointment?"

"All right." Lauren said. She wiped her sweaty palms on her pant leg as she waited to be connected.

"Mrs. Casey. This is Bob Haley. I can set up a time for you. When can you come in?"

"Soon, I'd like to get this out of the way."

"I had a cancellation for a one-thirty appointment today. Would that be convenient for you?"

"Yes, it would. Will it take very long?"

"Probably a little over an hour."

"That should work out just fine."

"Do you know where we're located?"

"No, I don't."

"Here's the address."

"Just a sec." Lauren got a pencil and pad and jotted down the information. "OKAY., I'll see you this afternoon."

She hung up the phone trembling. She was scared to identify Michael's body, and she was scared to take a polygraph test. She wondered if it was such a good idea. But then again, she knew she was innocent and she thought she shouldn't really have anything to worry about. She paced the kitchen floor, glanced at her watch, and decided to contact a funeral home. She picked up her phone and did a search for "funerals." She wondered how one goes about choosing a funeral home. Certainly a family doesn't shop for price at a time like this. She scrolled down the list and settled on a name she recognized from driving by the funeral home on U.S. 1. It was Ralph Lantz & Sons. She called the number and when a male voice answered, Lauren was mute.

"Hello. Hello. May I help you?"

Fighting back tears, she managed to say, "Yes. My name is Lauren Casey and I'd--I'd like to talk to you about funeral arrangements."

Chapter 5

Lauren walked through their home and inspected the rooms to make sure they were tidy for her parents' arrival. Typical of South Florida homes, theirs was four-bedroom, three-bath house built in the '70s, but thankfully boasted an updated kitchen and bathrooms. She busied herself by sweeping, vacuuming, and dusting. When she entered their master bedroom, Lauren stared at their king-size bed. Then she gazed at the dresser, the armoire, nightstands and finally Michael's briefcase that was next to wall by his side of the bed.

This is it, she thought. *I can't believe I'm not going to see him. This is all there is. Five and a half years with him. And the rest of my life without him. All our plans are gone. No children. This is the end. The end of my life with Michael. How can I go on without him? How can I live here in this house without him? The whole house is him.*

She felt so alone, but yet she felt his presence. *Are you here Michael? Is that possible? Was his spirit lingering, not wanting to leave her? He died a violent death at thirty-seven years old. Would someone pay for Michael's death with his own? Florida had the death penalty. But why was Michael killed? And who killed him? That was the mystery. The Michael she knew was honest and minded his own business. He was thoughtful and was smart. Is it possible to know someone for nearly six years and not know everything? Could a person be leading another life? Anything is possible. I just want answers. The case is now in the hands of the police. I know that some murders are never solved. I don't understand why Michael was murdered. I may never get an answer. And that is something I can't live with. I need to know who murdered him. And that person is going to pay for it.*

Lauren took one more look at Michael's side of the bed, walked out of the room, and closed the door.

A ringing telephone startled her out of reverie into the present. She found the portable on the couch and picked it up.

"Hello," Lauren answered, sitting down.

"Lauren Casey?" the voice asked.

"Yes?"

"This is Neil Adams from the *Miami News*. I'm a reporter and I'd like to get some information about your husband, Michael Casey."

By the time Lauren hung up, she was surprised at how many of his questions she answered. Adams had taken her off guard and she answered his questions, thinking somehow it would solve the mystery. She could only hope. She assumed the story would be in tomorrow's print and online edition and she wondered if any of the TV stations would be reporting the story as well. *If they come calling, I'll be prepared for them.*

Stopped at a traffic light, Lauren glanced at her watch. It was one o'clock and she was on her way to Miami-Dade Police headquarters to take the polygraph. Having just left the medical examiner's office, she wondered if it was such a good idea after all to have scheduled it for this afternoon.

Viewing Michael on the video monitor replayed in her mind. When the sheet was pulled back from her husband's face, she was not prepared for what she saw. This was her husband. And he was dead. There was no rise and fall of his chest. But somehow it didn't seem real. He's dead, she thought, he's actually dead. She remembered the lights in the room seem to blaze brighter than ever and then she felt faint. The attendant saw she was about to pass out and told her to sit down and put her head down at her knees. She did as she was told. He told her to breathe slowly. After a few minutes, she was able to sit upright. The attendant told her it was okay for her to stay as long as she wished. He handed her a paper cup of water. She nodded her head and with her voice cracking, "That's my husband, Michael Casey. When can I arrange for burial?"

The man told her that the autopsy would be done that afternoon and she could notify the funeral home to proceed with the arrangements. She wanted to run from the place, but all she could do was walk slowly across the parking lot to her car.

It took her thirty minutes to get to police headquarters. It was an impressive brick, glass block, and reflective glass building. She looked up at the windows and saw the cerulean sky and cotton candy clouds reflected in full color. Palms, lariope and pink impatiens ruffled in the breeze. She walked up to the front desk, identified herself, and stated her purpose. The officer checked his appointment calendar and called the examining officer to let him know she was waiting. She paced the lobby thinking if she could leave now if she wanted. As she got closer to the door, a tall man wearing a white dress shirt and striped tie greeted her. "Mrs. Casey? I'm Bob Haley, your polygraph examiner. How are you today?"

"Fair, thank you," Lauren said, extending her hand. They shook hands. He had a warm smile, deep brown eyes, and a firm handshake. She could detect a faint aroma of an aftershave, that seemed familiar, perhaps the one her Uncle Paul wore.

"If you'll follow me, I'll take you upstairs." Bob led the way to the elevator. They went to the second floor which gave her a birds-eye view of the conservatory. She followed him down a maze of hallways until they came to a cramped office. He invited her to sit down and he took a seat behind his desk. He explained to her that the test would probably take ninety minutes. But first, he wanted to do what he called a stimulation test. He pulled out a deck of cards, shuffled them and dealt out ten cards. He held the small pack of cards and fanned them out toward her. "Take a card, remember what it is, and then put it back with the rest. Don't tell me what it is, Okay?"

"Okay," Lauren said, taking the ten of hearts. She returned the card to the pack.

He handed her a printed sheet. "You heard of Miranda, haven't you?"

Lauren nodded yes.

"That's what this is in printed form. Please read it and sign it for me." Lauren read it carefully although she knew what to expect, having watched so many police shows on TV. She signed the form and handed it back to the examiner.

"Thank you. Okay, now, if you wouldn't mind removing your jacket and then taking a seat over there." Bob got up from his chair, excused himself as he squeezed by her and waited for her to take the seat by the polygraph machine.

Lauren slipped off her red gabardine jacket and lay it on the now vacant chair. She sat down by the polygraph machine. Sitting in this chair reminded her of the kind of chairs she sat in during her college days, but instead of having a wooden extension for writing, this one was on her left and it resembled a trough. It seemed natural to rest her left arm in it and she did.

"Good. Are you comfortable, Mrs. Casey?"

"Yes, and you may call me Lauren. How exactly does a polygraph work, anyhow?"

"Well, as I hook you up I'll explain. See this stretchy piece of tubing? It will expand and contract. We'll use two of them."

He connected the first piece of tubing around the top of her chest. "This first one measures thoracic breathing." He placed the second one around her rib cage. "The second one measures abdominal breathing." He then got a blood pressure cuff. "Would you extend your right arm for me?"

Lauren served up her arm like an obedient child. Bob wrapped the cuff around her arm above the elbow. "Good." He moved in front of her and attached metal clips to her index finger and middle finger on her left hand. "These sensors measure gastronomic skin response or GSR. That's all there is to it. A polygraph is actually a test of truth. You see, a person with something to hide has a fear of being found out. That causes stress and the body responds to stress in many ways. We're just measuring three of them --breathing, skin conductivity and blood pressure -- but there are actually twenty-six body functions that change during stress."

Lauren was thirsty but didn't have the nerve to stop the procedure to ask for a glass of water. She shifted her body in the chair. She watched the examiner place the cards face side up in a straight line on the desk on her left. He returned to his position at the polygraph machine at her right shoulder.

"Okay. We're ready to go. Will you please look at the cards? Are you comfortable?"

"Yes."

"Can you hear me all right?"

"Yes," Lauren said, uncrossing her legs.

"Whoops, you moved, didn't you? Let me make an adjustment. Okay. I'm going to name each card and ask if that's the card you picked. Please answer no to each question, even to the one you picked. Let's start."

Bob asked her about each card and each time she said no. She tried to make her voice sound the same each time she answered but realized she couldn't control it. In fact, her voice sounded odd to her. She also tried to keep her breathing even. When the examiner asked her about the ten of hearts, she thought she pulled that lie off pretty well. He then told her they would repeat part of the test and asked her to answer no to the king of spades, ten of hearts and eight of clubs. After he released the pressure in the cuff, he tore off the graph paper from the polygraph and showed it to her. She studied the peaks and valley. At the bottom of the graph, Bob had written in the card number for each question. The first time he asked her about the ten of hearts, there was what he called a camel's hump on the GSR and an increase in her breathing. He said that compared to the other cards, he would bet his money it was the ten of hearts. He was right, of course.

Lauren laughed. "My, I guess this thing works. I picked the ten of hearts."

"Good. Okay. Let's get started again."

Bob inflated the blood pressure cuff. Again he asked if she was comfortable. And then it began. Question after question. Some seemed relevant to the crime of Michael's murder and some didn't. Some sounded just like another with the addition of the time of day added to the question. He asked her if she ever committed an undetected crime and she thought she better answer yes. She figured taking home pens, pencils, paper clips and legal pads from work was considered petty theft.

He also asked her if she ever used force to make someone do something against their will. She thought that was a tough one to answer. She never used bodily force but she supposed she probably threw a tantrum as a kid to get what she wanted so she answered yes. An hour and a half later, she was free to leave. She was exhausted and her blouse was damp under her arms. The examiner said he would forward the results to Detective Dolan who would contact her. Escorting her down the elevator, he expressed his condolences and told her to be careful driving home. She was relieved the test was over. She knew she had nothing to do with Michael's murder, but what if her body made it look like she did? She pushed the thought out of her mind, realizing she was not concentrating on driving. She was on the way to the airport and she had to make sure she didn't miss the exit. As much as she tried, her thoughts were drawn to Michael like straight pins to a magnet.

Could he possibly have been mixed up with people I had no idea about, she wondered. *Maybe I didn't know him as well as I thought. Was there another woman? Who would have murdered him? I've got to find out who did this. I must.* She wrestled with one scenario after another until she saw the sign for the Miami International Airport.

Chapter 6

Lauren hustled down the concourse at Miami International Airport through the throng of pale faces burdened with their carry-on luggage and bulky winter coats. The Northeast was buried under three feet of snow so sunny South Florida offered a respite for winter-weary snowbirds. Florida's hospitality industry celebrated their arrival.

She spotted Betty and Warren walking toward her and she rushed to greet them. Lauren always thought her parents made a cute couple. Her father was a small man, only five-foot, six inches who at sixty still had a full head of dark brown hair with just a tinge of grey at the temples. Her mother was petite and wore her ash blond hair chin length in a classic bob. Her mother's blue eyes grew moist when she saw Lauren.

Lauren wrapped her arms around her mother and kissed her on her cheek. She took in the familiar fragrance of Shalimar and she was ten years old again. "Oh, Mom, I'm so glad to see you." She then turned to her father and hugged and kissed him, too. "It's been too long since I've seen you both."

"Six months since the wedding," Warren said.

Lauren's face clouded over and her father looked down sheepishly. "That's all right, Dad. You didn't say anything wrong," Lauren said, touching his arm. "Come on, let me take you to the escalator so you can go down to the baggage claim. I'll wait up here since Mom and Dad Casey are due in any minute."

"Warren, do you mind going down alone? I want to wait with Lauren," Betty said.

"No problem. I'll get the luggage and wait downstairs. I know the way. I'll see you in a few minutes," Warren said, walking ahead of them.

Betty turned to Lauren, "Oh, Lauren, I'm so sorry. It's just dreadful. Have the police given you any information?"

"No, Mom, in fact, I took a polygraph test this afternoon. Here, let me help you with your carry-on bag," Lauren said, taking the blue shoulder bag from Betty. "Gosh, what do you have in here, bricks?"

"Just the necessities. I don't understand. The police don't suspect you, do they?" Betty asked, her brows knitted together in concern.

"Well, they say it's strictly routine and purely voluntary. They want to eliminate family members as suspects." Lauren took her mother's hand in hers and gave it a gentle squeeze. "Don't worry, Mom.

"Did you have a lawyer present?"

"What for, Mom? I had nothing to do with it."

"I don't know. I guess I've seen too many movies."

Lauren stopped at the display board listing the status of arriving flights. "Let's see, Delta departure from Memphis. The plane has arrived. The gate is on this concourse so we can wait here for them."

"Have you taken care of the funeral arrangements?" Betty asked as she peeled off the periwinkle blue cardigan sweater revealing a matching sleeveless shell.

Lauren turned to face her mother. "Yes, I called the funeral home. The service is tentatively scheduled for one o'clock on Wednesday. When I have confirmation tomorrow the M.E. has released his body, I'll go there with Michael's clothes for burial. There's a contract to sign and I need to provide the life insurance policy Michael had through his employer."

Lauren let out a deep sigh and shook her head. Her eyes glistened as she fought back the tears. She didn't want to cry in public.

"I worry about you. I hope Michael had more than his employers life insurance policy," said Betty.

"We took out policies when we bought the house. Look, here come the Caseys now," Lauren said waving to the senior couple with silver grey hair ambling down the concourse. "Come on, Mom, let's go meet them."

Mother and daughter walked the short distance to Lauren's in-laws. Mom Casey was seventy-one and had a face that had softened with age. Her brown eyes looked sad through her large, wire-rimmed glasses. Dad Casey, at eight-one, still had the vigor of a man in his sixties. He was broad shouldered and still had a flat stomach. *Another Jack LaLanne,* Lauren thought, even with glasses.

"Mom and Dad Casey, I'm so sorry. And I'm so glad to see you both. I just wish... How was your flight?" Lauren asked, giving each in-law a gentle hug and a kiss on the cheek.

"Fine. It left on time but they didn't serve lunch. Just snacks and drinks. I've got that empty feeling," Mom Casey said rubbing her abdomen. She spoke in a soft, even tone as though she were sedated.

"Well, I can give you something to eat at the house to hold you over 'till we go out for dinner," Lauren offered.

"That's fine," Mom Casey said. "Betty, it's nice to see you again. Where's Warren?"

"Thank you, Bea, it's good to see both you and Eddie. I am so sorry. It's dreadful." Betty squeezed Bea's hand. "Warren went to baggage claim. We'll see him down there."

The group walked slowly down the concourse.

"Leonard and Julie will be flying in late tonight, Lauren. They said they'll get a taxi to our hotel. You'll see them tomorrow," Mom Casey said.

"Anyone else coming down besides my brother-in-law and sister-in-law?" Lauren asked.

"Yes. Uncle Seymour and Aunt Evelyn, Aunt Rachel and Cousin Barbara. Michael was always close to them," Mom Casey said, stepping on to the escalator and grabbing the handrail.

Lauren stood by the escalator as Dad Casey followed his wife, and then her mother and father. Having made sure each got on the escalator without mishap, Lauren finally stepped on.

At the bottom of the escalator Lauren looked at the baggage claim area. "You can get your luggage on Carousel 2, Dad Casey. I see my Dad waiting for us at Carousel 1 with theirs. Let's join him, and then I'll get the car while you wait for your luggage. I'll meet you all out front at curbside to pick you up. How does that sound?"

Dad Casey nodded. "Go right ahead. Be careful."

Lauren led the group to Warren and then headed out the automatic doors and crossed the lanes of traffic to the parking garage. She wondered where she should take her family to dinner and realized that she hadn't eaten all day.

It was ten minutes by the time she picked up her parents and in-laws at curbside. Lauren's Dad sat in the front seat with her and her mother and the Caseys sat in the back seat.

The ride back to Lauren's home was stop and go, typical of Miami's congested highways. Her mother said she had called all her cousins and her two aunts but none of them could fly down to Florida for the funeral. When Lauren asked about her favorite cousin Carolyn, her mother said she was unable to reach her and didn't want to leave a message on her answering machine with such dreadful news. Carolyn was always traveling. She was some sort of trouble shooter for a computer company. Lauren remembered that her cousin wasn't able to attend her wedding, either.

With both sets of parents together again, Lauren thought back to the day she married Michael. It was wonderful. She had never felt more secure and happy in all her life. Michael made a fabulous groom, so handsome in his tuxedo. And she had felt like a princess wearing her wedding gown. The ceremony was in the evening with the reception following at a first-class hotel in Coconut Grove. Surrounded by family and friends, she was having such a good time, she didn't want the party to end. They had spent their honeymoon night at the same hotel and when they made love she felt a spiritual connection to Michael. He was her soul mate.

"Lauren, what did your boss have to say when you called?" Warren asked.

"He was upset, naturally, but he told me to take the time that I need. I'll see how the week goes and try to go back next week. There's a video project I need to complete."

"For the cruise line?" Warren asked.

"No, Dad. It's for a real estate development company that builds primarily in the state of Florida, really big developments, but I hear they want to develop outside the state, going into Georgia. It's a major advertising account for the agency. They spend over two million dollars in advertising a year. With the new development, it should add another million to the media budget," said Lauren, parking in the driveway. "Okay, we're home. It's easier if you get out of the car here. Then I'll pull it in to the garage."

Lauren's mother and in-laws struggled to get out of the back seat. Warren helped Betty by reaching out his hand and pulling her out. Lauren did the same for Eddie who then helped Bea. They waited in the driveway until Lauren had parked and disabled the alarm. Her parents got their luggage out of the trunk and everyone followed her into the house.

"Mom, Dad Casey, did you want to take Michael's car and go to the hotel and check in now and meet us for dinner somewhere? Or would you rather wait here until we go to dinner?" Lauren asked.

"I'd just as soon go to the hotel after dinner," Mom Casey said, "if that's all right with you, Eddie. I've had enough traveling for the moment. Besides, I want you to show us your new home. All we've seen is the virtual tour from the listing agent."

Lauren realized her parents had only seen the virtual tour as well. "Of course. I'll put your luggage in Michael's car. Then the tour."

"I'll give you a hand," Warren volunteered.

Father and daughter transferred the suitcases to the grey Toyota Camry. When they returned to the house Lauren helped her father take the remaining luggage to the guest bedroom. It was located at the opposite end of the house from the master bedroom.

Warren turned to his daughter and put his hands on her shoulders. "Lauren. This is a horrible ordeal to have to go through. And I know we talked about it last night. But can you think of anyone who would have a motive for killing Michael? What about his friends?"

Lauren shook her head slowly. "I just don't know, Dad. Michael hung out with me. He didn't go out with any guys. I know it seems strange, but it's true. He really was a home body."

"No, there's nothing strange about it. I just wish I had a clue as to who killed Michael. He was such a fine young man. I just wish ..."

"I know, Dad." Lauren put her arms around him for a hug. Breaking free, she said, "I still can't believe he's gone. I know he is. I saw him, but it's not real."

Reaching for Lauren's hand, Warren said, "Come on. They're waiting. You need to give us the tour."

The two joined the others in the family room. It was a casual space with a couch, loveseat, and easy chair with an ottoman. The taupe Italian leather was brightened with throw pillow in navy, teal, and taupe. A teal chenille throw was draped on the arm of the couch. Opposite the seating area was a wall unit with a flat-screen TV on a low cabinet. On either side stood two oak cabinets that displayed books, framed photographs, and Lauren's collection of miniature vases and frog figurines. Glass topped end tables held matching lamps in antique bronze sculpted into a palm tree with two parrots. The matching coffee table was uncluttered except for two baskets. The remote controls were in one and the other corralled magazines and a novel. A spider plant hung from the ceiling in front of the sliding door to the patio.

"Let me show you around," Lauren said. She led them into the dining room with its formal cherry table and eight upholstered chairs in a sage green fabric. One wall featured a chiseled stone facade where tea light wall sconces accented the natural striation of the stone. An oiled bronze chandelier hung over the table casting light on an ikebana floral arrangement of three pink roses and a few blades of lariope.

"What a simple, but elegant flower arrangement," Bea said.

"I arranged it myself. I took a few floral arranging classes at the local florist. Out of all of them I really like ikebana. It's the way the Japanese do it. It's very structural and never boring."

"Did you change the stone wall?" Betty asked. "I thought it looked like something you'd see in a hunting lodge. The rocks were protruding and it looked rustic, unlike now."

"You're right. We had a stone mason come in and chisel it down so it's linear now. It was that or knocking it all down and putting up new drywall. I hated it before and now I love it."

"Me, too. I wondered what you would do with it, but of course I didn't say anything."

Lauren smiled. "Mom Casey, look in the china cabinet. Recognize anything?"

Bea turned around to look. "Ah, my La Belle China bowl I gave you when you got engaged."

"I remember you telling me the pattern was introduced in the 1890s. I've never owned an antique before. I'm happy to have it."

"Other women in our family have a single piece or two. Many pieces of the set were broken over the years. So that's it."

"I received a complete service for eight of my Lenox china. I packed it in those storage sets that I keep under the cabinet below. The platters are on display."

"And all your beautiful crystal stemware," Betty remarked.

"Those were wedding gifts from the partners in the ad agency. Eight water glasses and eight cordials."

"How generous!" Warren said.

"They're the best. I can't imagine working for anyone else."

They moved on to the living room which gave them a view of the landscaped front yard and street. Lauren remarked that the room was reserved for entertaining. The seating was two gray upholstered couches flanking an oversized cherry coffee table. On it were pillar candles and wood sculpture of a giraffe. Two matching chairs and two upholstered stools completed the grouping. A console housed a wine rack and wet bar along with storage space. On top of the console was a soapstone sculpture of a scallop shell.

"Nice sculptures," Dad Casey commented.

"We got them at the Coconut Grove Art Show. I love going, "Lauren said.

Lauren showed them the master bedroom and guest room that all had a pastel color scheme selected from the colors of each comforter. The third bedroom was set up as an office with built-in shelving and the fourth bedroom was empty.

Her parents and her in-laws looked at each other and remained silent each realizing that it most likely had been destined as a nursery. Then to break the awkwardness, each complimented Lauren on her decorating skills as they returned to the family room.

"What can I get you to drink?" Lauren asked, already knowing the answer. The Caseys would have sherry and her parents would have Scotch and soda with a twist. "The usual?"

Each nodded in agreement. Lauren went to the kitchen and returned with a tray of drinks, salsa, tortilla chips and unsalted pretzels. She served the drinks and put the tray on the coffee table with the snacks. After everyone was comfortable, Lauren raised her glass in a toast. "Here's to good health."

"Yes, Lauren, and to find out who killed Michael," Dad Casey said. "Promise me you'll keep us informed with every little bit of information you get."

"Of course." Lauren exchanged glances with her parents and in-laws and nodded. She swallowed her drink and closed her eyes, trying to stem the flow of fresh tears.

When she opened them, her mother took her by the hand and said, "Come sit by me. I have something for you."

"Mom, you didn't have to bring me anything."

"It's not something I bought. It's a letter from Michael that he sent to us after the wedding. I think you should have it. It speaks volumes about him."

Lauren slid the letter from the envelope and opened it. The date was a couple of weeks after their wedding day. It read:

Dear Betty and Warren,

Falling in love and marrying Lauren was the best thing that I have ever done. I thank you giving us your blessing.

And I thank you for raising a woman who has made my life complete. She's thoughtful and kind, and has an uncanny ability to read me. I know I can always count on her to follow through on anything she says she's going to. She has such integrity that I know I can trust her with my life. She just doesn't tell me she loves me. She shows her love for me in myriad ways. She would often quote you, Betty, "Actions speak louder than words."

I want to thank you for the incredible job you did in raising Lauren. You gave her an excellent education and a solid value system. You also gave her unconditional love and the confidence that she can do anything she sets her mind on. She also has a wicked sense of humor that puts me in my place when I get too full of myself.

I'm happy to have you both as my in-laws. I love your daughter and I promise to make her life with me a happy one.

With love and respect,
Michael

Lauren looked up from the letter and blinked away the tears. She put her hand to her mouth and gathered her thoughts. "That is so sweet. I had no idea he wrote to you."

Mom Casey said, "I don't want to intrude, but may I read his letter?"

"Of course. Here, the both of you can read it. I'm glad you gave me this letter, Mom. I'll cherish for as long as I live."

Chapter 7

When Ted Bomar awoke, his head throbbed and his mouth was as dry as cardboard from too many Stoli martinis the night before. At fifty-five years old, he was a heavy drinker and consequently suffered from hangovers every morning. But after a couple of acetaminophen, he was able to function in his role as CEO at Mirabella Corporation, one of Florida's leading real estate developers. Usually by lunchtime he felt fine. If not, he'd have a Bloody Mary or two at lunch to smooth over the ragged edges.

Ted sat on the edge of the king-size bed in his underwear. He spent the night on *Bomar's Bounty*, a 115-foot yacht he docked at Biscayne Yacht and Country Club. He originally bought the yacht for corporate entertaining, but couldn't resist using it as a trysting place. It never failed to impress women, the younger, the better. His bender began Sunday night and now it was Tuesday morning. He was secretly celebrating the demise of Craig Richards, his vice president at Mirabella Corporation. Ted had hired Craig two years ago from another developer whose principals went to jail for fraud. Craig was never indicted. Ted had figured the guy was smart and knew how to protect himself. But now Ted was more inclined to think that Craig was the whistleblower. He remembered first meeting Craig when he interviewed him. The guy had impressive credentials. A graduate of the Wharton School of Business, he had a great business mind. Ted didn't know if he'd ever find someone who was astute at feasibility studies and marketing as Craig, but he'd try. The guy knew too much and threatened to expose Ted which would blow the multi-million-dollar deal that he had pending.

He had no choice. He had to hire Julio to take him out. He figured he was putting Craig out of his misery anyway.

Ted considered Craig what they call a babe magnet, but it was for naught since the guy was still grieving the death of his wife. As far as Ted knew, the guy has been living the life of a monk. His wife Dena was killed in a car accident on her way home from the ob-gyn's office. She had just found out she was pregnant with their first child. Her passing was a double tragedy and Craig never got over it.

Ted thought Dena looked like a fashion model. She had long auburn hair, hazel eyes, and a figure he fantasized about. He had a hard time keeping his eyes off her the Sunday Ted had invited his management team and their spouses aboard for a day cruise.

He remembered when he first saw the yacht at the Boat Show in Fort Lauderdale. It had everything he ever wanted in a pleasure boat.

Each stateroom had its own private head featuring a marble vanity and bathtub, an entertainment center, luxurious carpeting and custom-built teak cabinets.

The main deck featured the main salon, dining area and bar, a galley hidden from the view of guests, and the master stateroom which had a full entertainment center.
When Ted saw the master stateroom, he was already sold. Jack, the yacht broker, took him back to the salon and opened the glass sliding doors to a deck where he could dine *al fresco*. Jack then led Ted up the spiral staircase to the boat deck.

"This is the bridge where the skipper takes command," Jack explained. "Here's bench seating where your guests can observe the skipper piloting the boat. Once the novelty wears off, they can retreat to the sky lounge which provides more intimate seating, a wet bar, and another entertainment center."

Ted followed Jack into the lounge which opened onto the fly bridge where there was more seating, an icemaker, refrigerator, and a gas grill. When Jack finished his sales pitch, he had also learned that *Bomar's Bounty* could cruise at twenty-five knots with a twenty-five hundred-mile range and open ocean capabilities. Much to Ted's chagrin, he hadn't cruised very far in it. The demands of his job as CEO limited his excursions to short trips to the Bahamas and some of the Caribbean Islands, which was great fun since the yacht had all the amenities: Jet Ski, fishing gear, snorkeling, and scuba gear. He chartered out the yacht whenever he could. With a captain and a crew of five, charters kept these people happy since they could also benefit from hefty tips. But chartering wasn't something that concerned Ted. He was quite happy having the yacht docked right where it was.

He thought about Esther. His wife of thirty years, she didn't question him when he spent nights away from home. He always forewarned her when he wasn't coming home, and he was discreet with his affairs as was his crew. They knew better than to let anything slip when Esther or any of their three adult children came aboard. Ted would have a lot to lose if Esther ever found out. She would divorce him and that was something he wanted to avoid, not just because it would be costly, but because he loved her. Life was comfortable with Esther. She was a good mother and never complained about the nights alone. She occupied herself reading or doing needlework in their luxurious estate in Gables Estates. In spite of his infidelity, Ted still had sex with Esther a couple of times a month. He thought Esther was happy. He was proud that he could provide her with a live-in maid, membership at the country club, a Mercedes, and a substantial allowance that allowed her to go on shopping sprees at whatever mall she selected. On occasion, she'd fly to New York and stay at the Plaza Hotel for a few days so she could shop Fifth Avenue. Sometimes he accompanied her on a weekend trip so they could take in a Broadway show together.

As a member of Miami society who headed many charitable organizations over the years, Esther had built a network with the wives of Miami's movers and shakers. In a sense, Esther opened doors of opportunity for her husband. With benefit concerts and charity balls to attend, Ted rubbed shoulders with the business elite. Once a social relationship was established, it was always easier to approach someone with a business proposal. Plus it was all good P.R. Invariably, the events were always covered in the newspaper's society page.

Yes, Esther was an asset. But she just wasn't very enthusiastic about sex. Ted lay back on the bed, remembering last night. This girl reminded him of the ones you see for cosmetic surgery commercials with huge breasts, full lips, and a perfect nose. He could still smell the perfume on the sheets, Black Opium, his favorite. He had given her a purse-size spray flacon of it when she arrived on the yacht. It was the first step in his seduction. After cocktails, a gourmet dinner and extolling her beauty, it was easy to bed her. Of course, he'd never see her again. He couldn't risk it. He didn't want to have to deal with a messy affair. Once he got what he wanted, he was done with her. There would be others. He knew women were attracted to him even though he was only five-foot-eight, and stocky. He could blame his German heritage, but he admitted his bulk came from too much fine dining and wining at Miami's finest restaurants and having the best chef aboard to cater to his every whim.

The urge to use the head forced him out of bed. He then washed his face and hands and ran a comb through his short blond hair. He leaned his hands on the marble vanity and stared into the mirror. The blue eyes looking back him were bloodshot. Ted opened the vanity drawer and took out the vial of Visine and the bottle of Tylenol. He put a drop in each eye and swallowed two caplets with water and thought, I've got to stop drinking so much, or I'll end up dead of cirrhosis.

He wrapped himself in a navy silk robe and walked barefoot to the main salon where a decanter of coffee and a silver tray of Danish pastries, bagels, and assorted muffins were on the teak dining room table. There also was a crystal pitcher of orange juice cradled in a bowl of ice. A floral centerpiece of white roses, ferns and baby's breathe perfumed the room. The table had been set for breakfast: Lenox china, Christofle silverware and a white damask placemat and napkin. The stewardess, a blond young enough to be Ted's daughter, appeared and poured coffee into the china cup.

"Thank you, Mary," Ted said, giving her figure the once over. She was wearing her white shorts uniform today which showed off her tanned legs to great advantage. Her straight, flaxen hair was pulled back in a ponytail.

"Would you like pancakes and sausage for breakfast or perhaps bacon and eggs?" She smiled and waited for his answer.

"No. What's on the table is fine. Thank you." Ted watched her leave the main salon and then turned his attention to the newspaper laying on the bar. He sat down on the barstool and went through the sections, wanting to read the business section first, but the headline and photo of a familiar face on the front page of the local news caught his eye. "Cyclist found dead in Grove" and a cutline under the photo identified the man as Michael Casey. Ted stared at the picture and his mouth dropped open. He was expecting the cutline to read Craig Richards. Not Michael Casey. Something was wrong. Horribly wrong.

The story said the victim had been found on a side street in Coconut Grove. The cause of death appeared to be a shot in the head. The police were investigating. The more Ted read, the more convinced he was that Julio had mistaken Casey for Richards. That means Richards is still alive! Acid burned in Ted's empty stomach. He looked at his watch. It was eight-thirty. He crossed the main salon to the telephone and called Craig Richards' office. Craig's assistant, Barbara, answered the phone and told him that Craig wasn't in yet. Ted asked if he had been at work yesterday. She told him no, that he had called in sick. Ted instructed her to call Craig's cell phone and leave a message to call him. He then dialed Craig's home number. The phone rang three times and then Craig's answering machine picked up. He hung up without leaving a message and dialed Julio's cell phone. The call went to voice mail and Ted left a message. Two minutes later, the phone rang.

"Mr. Bomar. It's Julio. What can I do for you, man?" The thickly accented Hispanic voice was cheerful.

"Julio, get your ass over here. I'm on the boat. Did you see the paper? You screwed up and you're going to have to fix it. Get over here. Now! Hear me? Now!" Ted bellowed into the receiver and disconnected the line.

He stared at the photo of Michael Casey and his face turned scarlet. "You pure bastard. You had to be in the wrong place at the wrong time. Shit. Now I've got to find Richards."

Chapter 8

When Lauren and her parents entered the chapel at the funeral home at one o'clock on Wednesday, she was surprised to see so many people had arrived early. Between Monday night and Tuesday morning, she had called everyone that wanted to know about the funeral.

She wondered if the media coverage would attract the curious to the funeral. There was the story in the newspaper Tuesday and the local TV news also reported the murder and urged anyone with information to call the police. Lauren refused to go on camera or even grant an interview to the reporters. Consequently, the information they reported was literally lifted from the newspaper story.

As she walked down the aisle, all heads turned to her, their faces acknowledging her grief. All of Michael's relatives were seated in the second pew while his parents sat in the front pew. Lauren took a seat next to Mom Casey and looked at the closed casket. There were several beautiful floral arrangements on both sides that perfumed the air, reminding Lauren of spring in New Jersey when her Dad's tulips and dogwood trees bloomed. She would be sure to look at the cards to see who sent them before she left.

On top of the polished rosewood casket was a framed photo of Michael and a floral spray of white roses. The funeral director gave her a choice of an open or closed casket, and she chose the latter. Michael's death was too gruesome and he was too young to die. She also knew that after the services, if they wished, she and her immediate family could have a private viewing before burial. Mom Casey dabbed at her eyes with a tissue and held Lauren's hand. Lauren looked at her, nodded, and thought how hard it must be to bury a son. Parents weren't supposed to outlive their children.

One by one, friends from work and Michael's co-workers from Goldsmith & Kline paid their respects and offered their condolences. It was all a blur. She thought it odd that she couldn't remember some of the names of these friends. Lauren managed not to cry until her best friend Judy came over to her and hugged her. Then the tears flowed. She pulled out a tissue from her suit jacket and blotted her cheeks. She inhaled deeply and slowly exhaled, trying not to break down in hysterics.

"Oh, Lauren, it just isn't fair," Judy said, kneeling down in front of Lauren so she could speak to her at eye level.

Lauren shook her head, her lips trembled trying to get her words out that were stuck in her throat. Finally she said, "Someone has to pay for this. I swear it."

"I hope they find him, Lauren. Now that the news has been on TV and in the papers, maybe someone will come forward with some information."

"I hope so," Lauren said as she looked at the people in the chapel wondering if anyone present could be capable of murder.

Chapter 9

Lauren felt a sense of relief with the funeral over. After the graveside service, she welcomed family, friends and neighbors to her home. Lauren had made a special point to invite her former landlord Stu and he had accepted. After all, he had helped her in their futile search for Michael. She also invited Michael's boss who cried openly at the grave.

Lauren looked over the buffet table set up in the dining room. It was laden with a variety of hot and cold foods, some were homemade by her neighbors, and other dishes were catered from the local supermarket and deli. With enough food to feed the entire neighborhood, she would be sure to allow them to take extra helpings home with them. Since the temperature was a delightful seventy-two degrees, Lauren had turned off the air conditioning and opened the windows and sliding glass doors. Many of her guests settled themselves out on the patio that offered additional seating at the rented tables and chairs. Lauren wandered into the kitchen where Cousin Barbara was making coffee in a borrowed thirty-cup coffee urn and Aunt Evelyn and Aunt Rachel were busy setting out strudel, cookies, miniature cheese cakes, and other baked goods on a sterling silver platter. The platter was a gift from her mother. It wasn't new, Betty explained; there hadn't been time to shop. She had received it as a silver wedding anniversary gift and wanted Lauren to have it.

Lauren looked around, noticing small groups engaged in small talk. She found the noise a comfort. These people were a distraction, and for now, that's what she needed. She wasn't quite ready to face a day all alone by herself, without Michael.

"Lauren, dear, can I fix you a plate?" Betty asked, putting her arm around her daughter's shoulder and pulling her close.

"I don't think so, Mom."

"I insist. You haven't eaten all day. Try a little something. You'll waste away to nothing."

"Not right now, in a little while. I have a terrible headache. I'm going to get some Tylenol; then I'll have something to eat," Lauren said, heading to the master bathroom. She excused herself through groups deep in conversation. The quiet of the bathroom was a sharp contrast to the rest of the house. She took the bottle of Tylenol from the medicine chest, shook out two caplets and swallowed them with water.

She heard the phone ringing and crossed the bedroom to her nightstand. She picked the phone up on the third ring. "Hello."

"Is this Lauren Casey?" the voice said in a low, even tone.

"Yes, it is. Who is this?"

After a long pause, the voice said, "I know who murdered your husband."

"What? Who is this? "

"My name is Craig Richards and I need to talk to you. In private."

"Wait a minute, Mr. Richards. I don't know who you are. Why should I talk to you?"

"Because I believe I'm the one who was the intended victim, not your husband."

"I don't understand," Laura stammered. "What are you trying to say?"

"Let me put it this way. I saw the picture of your husband in the newspaper and on the evening news. I'm a dead ringer for him. I'm sorry. I mean to say that I look like your husband."

"Are you saying someone intended to kill you and shot my husband instead? Is that what you mean?" Lauren asked. Her mouth went dry and she could feel her pulse throbbing wildly in her chest.

"Yes, that's exactly right. Look, I'm in danger. I'm sure the man who's behind all this has figured it out by now that I'm not dead. That means I'm being hunted. I'm sure you'd like to see the assassin go to prison. Can I meet you somewhere?"

"Look, this is all overwhelming. I buried my husband this afternoon and I have a house full of people. I'm not thinking real clearly. I need some time. Can I call you back?"

"No, I'll have to call you. I can't go home. It's not safe. I'll call you again, probably tomorrow. All right?"

"Listen. Why don't you just go to the police?"

"The man that ordered the hit is very wealthy and too powerful. He owns a lot of people in this city. I come forward and he knows where I am. I'd be a sitting duck. He'll make sure his button man will finish the job. I'd rather get everything all lined up first. With your help, I know I can put the gunman and this crook away for good."

"You think I can help?"

"Yes, I do."

"I don't see how I can."

"I just need a few minutes of your time. Please."

After a long pause she agreed, wondering if she was doing the right thing. "Shall I meet you somewhere?"

"Do you know where the Coral Gables Public Library is?"

"Yes, I do."

"Can you be there four o'clock tomorrow?"

"I guess. Where should I look for you?"

"By the magazines."

"How will I know you?"

"I look like your husband."

"Uh, right. Goodbye." Lauren returned the phone in its receiver and sat down on the edge of the bed, wondering what she should say or do. Surely, she thought, if I were to tell my parents, they would tell me not to get involved, to call the police. But Lauren knew that Richards was taking a risk calling her. Perhaps he was the key to putting the man who murdered Michael behind bars or given the death penalty. She had nothing to lose but time. She'd be in a public place and if she felt uncomfortable, she could leave. She couldn't help but worry. This was risky business.

"Oh, my dear Michael," Lauren whispered, massaging her forehead and temples. "What should I do?"

"Lauren, are you all right?" Betty said from the doorway. Do you want to lie down for a while? Everyone would understand."

"No, I'll be fine," Lauren said, getting up from the bed.

"Who were you talking to on the phone?" Betty asked.

"No one you know, Mom. Just someone who saw the news about Michael," Lauren said, knowing she was only telling her mother half the truth. She reached out to her mother who joined her in a warm embrace. "I'm so glad you're here for me. I don't know how I could get through this without you."

"I know, dear. I'm here as long as you want me to stay."

"Mom," Lauren said, breaking free and holding her mother's hands in hers. "Did you ever have someone mistake you for someone else? You know, like you were somebody's double?"

"Well, yes. A couple of times, now that you mention it. The first time was when I was a freshman at the University of Miami and I was walking to class. I was just a young girl of seventeen. All of a sudden, this huge guy, must have been a football player, came up to me, put his arms around me and bent me over backwards and kissed me, saying "Oh, Dixie, I love you!""

"What did you do, Mom?

"Well, I was so shocked that all I could say was 'But I'm not Dixie.' The guy almost dropped me on the ground, he was so embarrassed. He mumbled 'I'm sorry.' and took off like a bat out of hell."

"Did you ever see him again?"

"No, but I wished I had. He was real cute!"

"Mom!

"Well, he was."

"So did you ever find out who this Dixie was?"

"Yes, I tracked her down by asking friends if they knew her. It took some time, but eventually I got her phone number and called her. We agreed to meet in the Student Union."

"And did she look like you?"

"Yes, it was uncanny. We went in the ladies room and stood side by side facing the mirror to compare our faces. We were the same height and build, same hair color and style. You know shoulder-length with bangs. Same blue-green eyes. Naturally we saw that we weren't identical but we could understand someone mistaking us."

"Did you become friends with her?"

"No, but I did join the same sorority she belonged to. She transferred to another college after the fall semester. Turned out she missed the boyfriend back home too much."

"You said this was the first time."

"Yes, there was another incident when I was still in college. I was on Key Biscayne playing tennis and someone mistook me for another woman."

"Was it Dixie?"

"Oh, no. It was another person, but I don't remember her name now. Then just last month in a restaurant, I was having lunch with a girlfriend and this man came over and said 'Hi, Renee.'"

"Maybe he was just trying to pick you up."

"Me? No I don't think so," Betty said, blushing.

"Oh, come on, Mom, you're still a pretty woman, " Lauren said, managing a smile.

"And you're still the sweetest daughter a mother could ever wish for. If you're up to it, Lauren, let's go join the others."

"All right. I'm just getting tired."

"I think we all are. It's been a long day for everyone so I think your company will be leaving in a little while."

Lauren followed her mother into the family room, thinking about her rendezvous with Craig Richards. She was nervous about meeting him, knowing that this is the man that should be dead, not her Michael.

Chapter 10

Lauren awoke to breakfast aromas of coffee, toast, and bacon. Never ones to sleep late, her parents were up and her mother made herself at home in Lauren's kitchen.

She looked at the empty space next to her in the bed and she thought of Michael. He was always an early riser; even on the weekends he'd be up first to make Lauren breakfast. He prided himself on being a superb short order cook, managing to get bacon, eggs and toasted bagels on the table all at once. She always made a big fuss over his efforts, because she really did appreciate his help in the kitchen. She found him thoughtful in other ways, too. Oftentimes on a weeknight, if he had gotten home before her, Michael would set the table, light candles, and make a salad. All that Lauren had to do was prepare the main entree and a side dish. She really enjoyed cooking for Michael. He always made positive comments on what she had cooked and he was eager to try new recipes she found in magazines, the internet or from a new cookbook she had picked up at the local bookstore. After dinner, he always cleared the table. Thinking about the day-to-day living that she cherished with Michael brought heaviness in her heart. *How would she live without Michael?* she thought. The idea made her shudder.

Lauren got out of bed and went to the bathroom to take a sedative. Judy had given Lauren her prescription bottle. Lauren had protested at first, because it was not prescribed for her, but she figured the pills would ease her anxiety so she could get through the day. She looked at her watch. She was surprised that she slept until nine o'clock. She brushed her hair and pulled on her robe. When she looked at herself in the mirror she saw a face that was pale and joyless. With a deep sigh, she turned and headed toward the kitchen.

Her mother poured her father a second cup of coffee. He sat at the kitchen table with the morning newspaper in his hands. He looked over the top of it and said, "Good morning to you."

Returning the coffee pot to the warming element, Betty said, "Good morning, Lauren. I'm glad to see you slept a little later. You needed the rest. Can I fix you some breakfast?"

"In a few minutes, maybe. Just some juice and coffee for now. How are you? Did you both sleep well?" Lauren went to the refrigerator to get the grapefruit juice.

"Not too bad, except for this pain in my right shoulder. Once the ibuprofen kicks in, I'll be all right." Betty got a mug out of the cabinet. "Shall I pour you a cup of coffee?"

"Yes, thanks Mom. Would you like some juice?"

"No thank you. I've already had a glass."

"I'll have a bagel, but you sit down, Mom. I'll get it."

Her father put the paper down. "What time are your in-laws coming over?"

"About eleven this morning. They said they were going to call Detective Dolan this morning to see if he had any suspects. After that, they were coming here," Lauren said. She finished her juice and sipped her coffee.

"Have you heard anything more about the case?" Warren asked.

"Actually, no. But I was expecting a call from Detective Dolan about making a formal statement. I told him that I would come in today. I'd like to make it this morning to get it over with."

"You're not worried about it, are you?" Betty asked.

"Well, yes. This whole thing is upsetting. I hope I don't break down crying hysterically."

"You'll do fine," Betty said. She got up and cleared the breakfast dishes.

"Dad, may I see a section of the newspaper?" Lauren asked.

"Here, take the whole thing. I'm through reading it. If you ladies will excuse me, I'm going to walk around your garden. It's such a nice day."

"Go right ahead, Dad."

Warren got up from the table and let himself out to the yard through the patio.

Lauren began reading the local news section. A headline caught her attention. "Broward Center expected to expand."

The publicly funded school in the Broward County school system was founded in the late sixties as an education center dedicated to developing innovative teaching methods which could then be disseminated throughout the county. Children in grades kindergarten through twelve were bused from all over the county to the campus. To be admitted to the school, parents put their children's names on a waiting list when they were born with the hope that someday they would receive a letter granting them the privilege of attending Broward Center. There was no entrance exam. Children were chosen with an eye to mirroring the population of Broward County so it would not upset the racial balance of their home school. The four schools that made up the Broward Center were two elementary schools, one middle school and one high school. The high school excelled with high test scores on standardized tests, but gained national recognition for being the sixth best public high school in the nation by a national magazine. The yardstick in ranking schools was the ratio of Advanced Placement and International Baccalaureate exams given in the year divided by the number of graduating seniors. AP and IB courses are rigorous college-style classes that require students to pass nationwide tests for credit. Consequently, Broward Center high school students believed their applications to the college to which they applied got more than a cursory glance. And they did. Many high achievers were accepted and awarded full scholarships to some of the finest colleges and universities in the country, including the prestigious Ivy League schools. The article stated that the Broward County School District was considering building a second Broward Center campus in north Broward County. The existing one was located in the southeastern end of the county so children living in the north end didn't get home from school until six o'clock. Having a north campus would allow children in the vicinity the option to transfer to the new site. Moreover, it would alleviate overcrowding at the middle and high school levels. The task at hand was finding a suitable site.

Lauren remembered having a discussion with Michael about moving to Broward County after reading about the Broward Center on several occasions. Since they hoped to have children, good schools were a priority. They also felt Broward offered better real estate values than Miami-Dade County, had a lower crime rate, and Broward's schools fared better when it came to national test score averages. They had driven from Miami one weekend and were impressed by the clean streets and landscaped medians. Even vacant lots had their lawns mowed and were kept free of debris. It was a pity, but vacant lots in Miami-Dade County became an overgrown dump site for all kinds of trash. It was an eyesore, but city officials seemed to have other priorities.

Lauren put the paper down and stared at nothing. She tried to push the thought of Michael out of her mind, but she gave in to it and began to cry softly.

Betty heard her sobs and put her arms around her daughter. She rested her head on her daughter's and said, "Lauren, I'm so sorry."

"Mom, I'll was just thinking about Michael—that I'll never has his children," Lauren cried. "Whoever killed him has taken that away from me."

Betty remained silent as the tears flowed down her daughter's pale cheeks. The telephone rang, interrupting their mutual grieving.

"Will you answer that for me, Mom?"

"Sure," Betty said, leaving her daughter. "Hello. Yes, Lauren Casey is here. May I tell her whose calling? Detective Dolan. Just a minute, please."

Covering the mouthpiece of the telephone, Betty said, "Can you talk, Lauren or shall I tell him you'll call him back?"

"No, it's all right. I'll take it," Lauren said, taking a deep breath and exhaling slowly. After she composed herself, she took the receiver from her mother.

"Good morning, Detective. Yes, that's fine. I'll be there at eleven."

Lauren hung up the phone. "Mom, can you keep the Caseys busy when they get here? I'm going downtown to make a statement. I have to be there at eleven and it shouldn't take too long. I'll be home for lunch."

"That's no problem. I'm sure they'll understand, but why don't you give them a call at their hotel this morning."

Lauren walked over to her mother and wrapped her arms around her. "You know, I don't know what I'd ever do if anything ever happened to you or Dad. I love you both so very much." Fresh tears began to flow.

Betty held her daughter tightly. "Nothing is going to happen to us Lauren. Don't worry about that now. We're here for you. And if you feel lonely and don't want to stay here, you're welcome in our home.

Lauren pulled away to look at her mother. "You really mean that?"

"Of course I do."

"I'll give it some time and see how I feel. I have a good job here and good friends. But this house without Michael, I just don't know. Moving could mean starting fresh."

"It's something to think about it."

"Yes, I'll let you know." Lauren hugged her mother once more, grateful that she had options.

Chapter 11

Lauren pulled into the parking lot at the Coral Gables Public Library and parked under the shade of an ancient oak tree. She was ten minutes early for her rendezvous with Craig Richards, having made good time driving into the Gables from Kendall. At this point she was tired of driving since she had gone to Miami-Dade Police headquarters in the morning so Detective Dolan could take her statement. She told him exactly what happened Sunday night, which now seemed like a very long time ago. Afterwards, she asked him if they had any leads or suspects. He said he was working on the case and that her polygraph was inconclusive. She simply said, "Oh," not wanting to pursue the subject. She figured if he asked her to take another test that would be the time to hire an attorney. She wondered if he suspected her, but she didn't ask. She didn't need anything else to worry about.

She now sat in her car, her hands trembling, her mouth dry, and her stomach churning. *What the hell am I doing here?* Lauren thought. She looked around the parking lot and saw only a few other cars. She wondered if Craig Richards had arrived yet. She got out her car, locked it and looked around as she walked to the entrance of the library. The automatic doors opened as she approached them and a blast of Artic air hit her in the face. Lauren shivered and wished she had brought a sweater. As she walked toward the magazine racks, Lauren's eyes scanned the library for the man that had the face of her dead husband. Instead, she saw two senior ladies checking out their books at the front desk and in the juvenile literature section, she noticed two young mothers and their toddlers making their picture book selections. Lauren selected *Southern Living* from the display of magazines and sat down in an arm chair against the wall. She checked her watch. It was three-fifty-eight. Too nervous to read, she flipped through the pages, pausing to look at the photography. Part of her wanted to run out of the library, afraid of what she would learn from Craig Richard's, afraid to see her dead husband's double. But the other part of her, the part that wanted justice, held her in her seat. She wiped her sweaty palms on her denim jeans and leaned over to get a breath mint out of her purse. When she straightened up and put the lozenge in her mouth, Craig Richards was standing in front of her, holding a pile of art books.

"Lauren? I'm ..."

"Yes, I know who you are." The knot in Lauren's stomach got tighter and she began to cough. She knew she was going to be sick. She got up from the chair, grabbed her purse, and covered her mouth. "I'll be back. Excuse me." Lauren dashed to the ladies room where she barely made it to the toilet. Her whole body heaved as she spilled the contents of her stomach. When she had nothing left, she flushed the toilet and leaned against the stall wall. Her eyes were wet with tears and she dabbed at them with the rough toilet tissue. She went to the sink where she washed her hands and using her cupped hands, she rinsed her mouth. She looked at herself in the mirror thinking this business with Craig Richards was dangerous. And she knew she still had a choice. She could walk out of this room and go directly to her car or she talk to Craig Richards. Lauren turned off the faucet and dried her hands. Her inner voice told her she had to do whatever it took to find Michael's killer.

Chapter 12

As Lauren approached, Craig Richards got up from his chair. He was a spitting image of Michael. He was wearing jeans, a navy pocket T-shirt and brown topsiders without socks. He had a light complexion, brown eyes and he wore his dark brown hair short, combed straight back. She noticed the beginnings of a five o'clock shadow along his jaw line.

"I'm sorry, Lauren, for the shock," Craig said.

"It's quite unnerving to look at you." Lauren turned away. "Let's go sit over at that table."

"After you."

Along one wall of windows of the library, there was a study area with several wooden tables that could accommodate four. They selected a corner table and sat across from one another. No one occupied the other tables so they had privacy. Craig glanced around the room and then spread the art books out on the polished oak table to give the appearance that they were doing research together. Lauren was mesmerized looking at his face. "It's simply amazing, your face—I—I just can't believe my eyes," Lauren stammered.

"I can imagine how you're feeling. It's very upsetting for me to know that another man is dead because he happened to look like me."

"Look, I'm having a hard time dealing with this. I don't know what to say so why don't you fill me in on who you are and what you think happened, okay?" Lauren whispered.

"All right. For what it's worth, I'm thirty-nine, I live in Coconut Grove. I grew up in Pennsylvania and I'm the oldest of five children. I'm a graduate of the Wharton School of

Business, got married when I was twenty-five to Dena, a school teacher. We would have been married thirteen years, but she was killed in a car accident five years ago. She was pregnant when she died."

"I'm terribly sorry," Lauren said seeing the pain in his eyes.

Craig shook his head. "I told you that because I want you to know that I have an idea of what you're feeling right now. It's something you don't get over. A tragic death. It's like having the rug pulled out from beneath your feet. I still have a lot of anger inside. You see, Dena and I had a good life together. She wasn't just my wife. She was my best friend. I'm a better man because of her. She was incredibly easy-going. We traveled a lot, went to jazz concerts, collected fine art, and went to the nicest restaurants. We were even thinking about buying a sailboat until— "Craig was lost in thought for a moment. "Well, enough of that. I'm sure what you really want to know is why someone would want to kill me. I'll try to explain. I've been working for Mirabella, the real estate developer, for two years. I'm vice president responsible for marketing."

Lauren's eyes widened in surprise. "Mirabella! I work for an ad agency and Mirabella is a client."

"Really? Sindelar Newton and Partners. Where have they been hiding you?" Craig asked, his eyebrows knitted together.

"You deal with Bill Parsons, the account executive. That's his job, client contact. I'm a creative type and we usually don't have direct contact with the client. You know, they're afraid a client might criticize our work and bruise our fragile egos. On occasion, we'll meet with a client for an input session. But that's usually when we land a brand new account and the agency wants to introduce the team who will be working on their account. That's the time we get as much information as we can about the client's product or service and learn about their marketing objectives."

"So I guess you started working for the agency after we became a client," Craig offered.

"That's right."

The Deadly Game

Craig looked upward to the ceiling and Lauren could imagine the wheels in his mind working at some thought.

"Craig," Lauren said, the sound of his name seeming odd to her. She lowered her voice. "Working for Mirabella doesn't explain why someone wants to kill you."

"Let me continue. I know too much. My boss is Ted Bomar, the CEO of Mirabella. He's been negotiating to sell some land to the School Board of Broward County for a new school complex. Have you read anything about the Broward Center?"

Lauren nodded her head yes. "I read an article about it this morning."

"The deal is worth millions," Craig continued. "But the problem is the land he wants to sell is a contaminated site. And Ted has no intention of revealing the fact."

"Wait a minute. Contaminated? With what?" Lauren wanted to know.

"Various toxic chemicals. If I started to name them all, you'd think I was reading from a chemistry book. The problem goes back to the late fifties when the site was owned by the Bayberry Chemical Company for a pesticide plant. The plant made many pesticides, including DDT, which you know was banned by the EPA because of links to cancer. Then in the mid-seventies, there was a fire at the plant. Drums of chemicals and bags of pesticides were destroyed. What remained of the plant and bags of water-soaked pesticides were buried there in a pit. As things go, the company had financial problems and the site was abandoned. Two years after the fire, Mirabella bought the property and leased the land to McKinley Group, a wholesaler that repackages solvents. Then in the early eighties, McKinley Group was acquired by another company and eventually the place was shut down. Drums of chemicals that were remained were buried there. Who knows if any of the toxins seeped into the groundwater? Since that time, the area has been urbanized and it's out of the way for industry. So the site is a vacant lot."

Craig paused. "Are you aware of the Superfund Program?"

"Vaguely."

"In 1980 Congress created the Superfund Program to pay for the worst hazardous waste sites in the nation when the original polluters could not be determined. Disposing of hazardous materials is not cheap. I recently read about a well field in Broward County that supplies drinking water to Fort Lauderdale residents. It was contaminated by waste oil in an industrial park about a mile south of the well. Now the EPA must figure out how to contain the pollution to make sure it doesn't spread or seep deep into the Biscayne Aquifer and then decide on the best method for removing the contaminated soil. The EPA will go after the property owners to recover the money spent on the investigation and cleanup which could cost two million dollars." Craig shook his head and then continued. "Ted knew he had a problem and he had this idea. He knew the site would cost at least a million dollars to clean up."

"A million dollars! Why does it cost so much?" Lauren asked.

"Because of manpower and equipment. It's a long process and there are several ways to clean up a site. You can excavate the contaminated material and haul it to a federal-approved hazardous landfill or incinerator. Or you can clean it up in place using such esoteric techniques as soil gas extractor or bioremediation. But back to Ted. Rather than go to the expense of cleaning up the site, he made a decision to use the land as an illegal dump site and make some money from it," Craig said.

"I don't believe it. That's disgusting," Lauren said.

"I agree. But he did get lots of customers."

"But why?"

"Money. I told you it costs lots of money to dispose of hazardous waste. A licensed hazardous waste disposal company will typically charge a thousand dollars per barrel. That's a lot of money to small family-owned businesses such as dry cleaners, auto repair shops, printers, and pest exterminators. Ted charged much less.

"Is this still going on?" Lauren shook her head in disbelief.

"No. He operated the site for about a year and gave it up. He eventually thought it was too risky."

"It's bad enough he ran the risk of chemicals seeping into our water source. And now he wants to sell the land to the School Board. Is this man nuts?" Lauren let out a sigh in disgust.

"I would say so. Yes. Ted actually thinks he can get away with it."

"But he can't, can he? I mean, wouldn't the soil have to be tested before someone could build on the property? I'm no expert, but with all you hear these days, I would think that's what happens."

"Actually, you're right. In most cities in South Florida, before you can get a building permit, you have to have soil borings done. And if you're a smart buyer, you'll get the job done before you buy a piece of property. Otherwise, as the owner, you're then responsible if there's a problem. You'd end up paying for any clean up."

"Wouldn't the school board do that? Do the soil borings? Is Ted thinking that they wouldn't be smart enough to do it?"

"Oh, sure. He's anticipated that they'll do environmental tests. After all, the school board was burned once last year. They bought a ten-acre site for a primary learning center and an elementary school. Then before building, tests were done which turned up wood, metal, concrete, plastic, and methane gas. The sellers, who also happen to be developers like Ted, had a county permit to bury construction debris on the site, but -- according to the newspaper -- the building manager wasn't aware it had been used as a dump site. So Ted thinks he can get around any problems. He believes he can bribe the school board's building manager or the city engineer to falsify a report."

"Unbelievable! Do you think he could pull it off?"

"Not a chance. I intended to make the building manager aware of the situation if Ted proceeded. I told Ted that," Craig said. He took in a deep breath and exhaled slowly. "I thought I had talked Ted out of going through with his plan. I told him to clean up the site. God knows he can afford it. I think it's just a question of greed. I swear I didn't think the guy was nuts enough to want to have me killed over the situation."

"How did you find out about this in the first place? Is it obvious it's contaminated by looking at the site?"

"Ted told me about it after too many martinis. The guy drinks like a fish. And he's an egomaniac. To answer your second question, no, it's not obvious to look at. It's just land."

"I take it you haven't been back to the office?" Lauren looked Craig straight in the eyes.

"Damn right. Turned out I wasn't feeling so hot on Monday so I called in sick. Tuesday is when I saw the story in the paper with the picture of your husband. That's when I got the hell out of my house. I know Ted reads the papers and watches TV. I'm sure Ted put surveillance on my house so I don't dare go home. "

"Where are you staying?" Lauren asked.

Craig looked over his shoulder. "Just some dive--a no-tell motel on Calle Ocho, you know, Southwest Eighth Street in Little Havana. I don't feel real comfortable staying there. I need to find another place."

Lauren looked outside through the windows of the library. She noticed the long shadows cast by the trees. She knew it would be starting to get dark soon.

Craig leaned forward. "Don't get me wrong. I'm not suggesting —no, I wouldn't want to put you in jeopardy. I can't stay in any one place in this area for long."

Lauren looked at Craig and thought for a moment before saying, "Maybe you should get out of town. I have an idea. My cousin owns a condo in Naples, right across from the beach. She lives in New Jersey most of the year so she uses it as a rental during the tourist season. She may not have anyone in there now. "I'll call her and ask her if you could stay there."

"No, I couldn't. I don't want to put you to any trouble."

"No problem. But I was just thinking. I can see why you don't want to go to the police. You'd have to surface and make an accusation. You don't know who Bomar's friends are. But why shouldn't I go to the police?

"You mean go to them and tell them what I just told you? Without any evidence, you don't have a case. They wouldn't arrest Ted. No, bear with me. Together I think we can get the goods on Ted to put him behind bars."

"All right for now. It scares the hell out of me, quite frankly. I don't know you, but it looks like fate has thrown us together. You're the link to my husband's murderer and I want to see this guy Ted, not just behind bars, but frying in the chair at Starke. Maybe the two of us can figure a way to convict Bomar. But before we get into that, there is something I'm trying to figure out." Lauren leaned forward in her chair.

"What's that?"

"My husband was riding his bike in the Grove when he was murdered. Now you said Ted arranged for his murder, thinking it was you, of course. So how did this hit man know where you'd be or think you'd be?" Lauren asked.

"Well, Ted knew I rode my bike every weekend through the Grove. He could have had the hit man tail me to see what time I usually go, which happens to be mid-afternoon. And if you're biking through the Grove, most people just follow the bike path. Unfortunately for your husband, I didn't go biking Sunday because I felt like I was coming down with the flu. I told you I didn't go in to work Monday," Craig explained hoping to offer Lauren some measure of comfort.

"So I guess the killer just sat and waited until Michael rode by and followed him," Lauren sighed and slumped down in her chair.

"I'm really sorry, Lauren. I wish——."

Lauren interrupted. "It's really not your fault. I know we can't change the fact that Michael is dead. But we can do

something about Ted Bomar. We just need to work out a
plan."

Chapter 13

Lauren dreaded Monday mornings and this one was even worse since it was raining. She knew she would be late for work since the traffic was slow heading north along U.S. 1 into downtown Miami. There were long stretches of three-lane road where the right lane was flooded, forcing motorists to either work their way out of the lane to the center lane or slow down to a crawl to get through the water. This was not unusual and she wondered why city engineers never fixed the drainage problem.

The windshield wipers were on high speed and Lauren could barely see the cars in front of her. She gripped the wheel and leaned forward to try to see through the downpour. She was tense and thought about turning around and going home, but she knew it was going to be a short workday since she would be leaving mid-afternoon to take her parents to the airport.

After her meeting with Craig at the library Thursday afternoon, Lauren knew she had little time to spare so it was important to get back to work. Over dinner Friday night with her parents and in-laws, she told them she thought it best that she go back to work Monday. She had spent a week in mourning and thought she needed to get her mind on other things to help her work through the grieving process. All were in agreement that it was a good idea for her to get on with living. Each couple then discussed when they should leave and return to their respective homes. Lauren's mother offered to stay longer, but Lauren convinced her she'd be just fine on her own. Besides, she thought, with what I have to do, I don't want to have to make up lies. The Caseys decided that they would leave Sunday night. Lauren thought they were incredibly strong people and loved them. She hoped she could still keep a relationship going with them, but she knew a lot of that happening depended on her keeping in touch with them on a regular basis. Lauren had suggested that they spend the rest of the weekend taking in some of Miami's tourist attractions. On Saturday, they went to the Seaquarium on Key Biscayne to see the dolphins. On Sunday after lunch, they went to Fairchild Tropical Gardens. It was a beautiful afternoon and there were many families taking in the splendor of the landscaped grounds. The Caseys were delighted with the pink flamingos and the Albino peacock while Lauren's mother thought the sausage tree was just too comical. By Sunday night, Lauren suggested that they have a quiet dinner at home. She reheated the lasagna that her neighbor had brought over after the funeral Wednesday and she made a salad. Over coffee and dessert, they looked at Lauren's photo albums that were filled with pictures of Michael and her. On one hand, she found comfort in looking at the pictures; on the other, she was heartbroken. The pictures also reminded her of Craig Richards. It was an eerie feeling.

The rain had finally let up so she reduced the speed of the wipers to normal. Lauren leaned back and relaxed her grip on the wheel. She had the radio on and a screaming commercial for a car dealership came on. She knew of the ad agency that produced these spots. The owners of the firm were two ex-disc jockeys who insisted that their screaming announcers brought warm bodies into the showroom. Irritated, she switched to her favorite oldies station on the radio. The song that played was an old one, from the early 70s she thought. It was Johnny Nash's "I Can See Clearly Now" about the rain being gone.

Lauren hoped there would be brighter days ahead.

The rain was now just a drizzle and Lauren put the wipers on the lowest speed. She was now on Brickell Avenue and she turned right at Southwest Eighth Street to go over the bridge to Brickell Key. The agency had their offices in the

Courvoisier office tower overlooking Biscayne Bay. Lauren was fortunate to have an office with a window and the spectacular view spoiled her for a job anywhere else. She pulled into the garage and found her reserved parking space. She was grateful that she could park under cover. By now most of the reserved spaces were occupied by those workers who had more enthusiasm for Mondays than Lauren.

Lauren took the elevator to the seventh floor and opened the glass door to the reception area. The offices were decorated in shades of pale shades of green, blue, and grey. Potted plants and framed watercolor paintings of Florida flora adorned the walls. One wall had floor-to-ceiling windows offering panoramic views of the sparkling bay.

She smiled and nodded at Lucy, the receptionist at Sindelar Newton & Partners, who was busy answering one call after another. She put her fore finger up indicating for Lauren to wait a minute. Lucy also was a newlywed. Her husband was an account representative from the local Spanish television station. It was love at first sight for the couple when Julio called on the agency to meet with the media buyer. Lauren recalled that Lucy once confided in her that she was worried that she was pregnant. Lauren was surprised that the woman wasn't using birth control since she hadn't gotten married yet. Lucy confessed that she was a devout Catholic, so it was against church doctrine. The logic of it didn't make sense. Wasn't premarital sex against church doctrine, too? It must've been a huge relief to Lucy when she finally had her wedding.

Lucy ended her call and said, "Lauren, I'm sorry. It's such a shock."

Lauren nodded, unable to speak and looked upward trying to ward off an avalanche of tears. She knew she had to compose herself or she should go home. Lauren did her usual deep breath exercise to calm herself, then said, "It's hard to talk about it just now. Later, okay?"

Lucy left her seat and embraced Lauren. She whispered in her ear, "Everyone here is praying for you." Lauren broke the embrace and forced a small smile.

Feeling self-conscious, she hurried to her office and said good morning to those co-workers who weren't either on the phone or engrossed in a meeting.

As she sat down at her desk and put her purse in the bottom drawer, she looked up to see Greg Sindelar in the doorway. He had closely cropped brown hair speckled with gray and a neatly trimmed brown beard. He pushed his wire-framed glasses back up on his nose. Highly intelligent, he had the air of a university professor rather than that of an advertising executive. "Welcome back, Lauren. How are you?"

"Honestly? Devastated. But I'll be all right. I guess. And how are you? Did you get Jim Lawrence to come in and freelance?" Lauren hoped that he had and given him some of the garbage assignments that had been piling up on her desk.

"I'm fine and yes, I had Jim come in for two days. It was enough time to clear the decks, so you can spend your time on the Mirabella presentation video. There's a short status meeting at ten o'clock. You don't have to go if you don't want to. Just read the status report that was emailed to you. If you have any problems regarding deadlines, see me. Also, Lauren, this is your first day back. I'll understand if you don't want to work a full day. See how the day goes. Just let me know if you need more time. I have to make sure deadlines are met, and I can call Jim in if need be. So, if there's anything you need, just holler." Greg smiled at Lauren. "And if you want someone to talk to, my door is always open. You know that."

Lauren managed a small smile. "I really appreciate your understanding, Greg. As a matter of fact, I need to leave this afternoon at three to take my parents to the airport. But I'll take the Mirabella file home to review and get started on the outline."

"No problem. I know you'll do a bang-up job. You always do. Why don't you get yourself some coffee? Lucy brought in a bag of fresh bagels. With this crew, you better get to them before they're all gone."

"Thanks, Greg. I just want to check my voice mail for messages first."

"All right. You know where I am if you need me," Greg said.

Lauren admired Greg. He was a family man who married his college sweetheart after getting his bachelor's degree from the University of Florida. He had two boys, born two years apart and attending elementary school. His wife was a stay-at-home mom and Lauren liked her instantly when she was invited for dinner their house in South Miami. They had a treasure trove of Americana antiques and collectibles artfully displayed. Lauren's favorite was the Victrola phonograph

Lauren turned to her phone to retrieve her messages. There were only three messages, one from Marshall Taylor who was the voice-over announcer she planned to use for the Mirabella video. He expressed his condolences and also asked that she let him know when she reserved studio time to record the script. She jotted down his name and number with a reminder to call him when she had the information. The other two were hang-ups which she thought was odd, considering hers was a business office.

Lauren dialed Liz Caldwell's extension, the broadcast producer for the agency.

"Liz, it's Lauren. I was going to get some coffee and come to see you about the production schedule for Mirabella. Is that okay?"

Lauren knew she didn't have to ask because Liz was never too busy to stop for her, even if it meant she had to squeeze two day's work into one. Liz was single, twenty-six years old, very attractive with long blond hair and brown eyes. She reminded Lauren of a doe, vulnerable and fragile in the wild. Liz came from one of Miami's oldest and wealthiest families and had inherited a small fortune from her grandmother. Lauren sensed that Liz worked to have a sense of purpose to her life. And work she did. Long hours that sometimes stretched into the night. Lauren wondered if Liz found any time to date.

"Oh, sure, Lauren. Any time."

Lauren hung up the phone and went to the kitchen. She found a mug in the cabinet and poured herself some coffee and added almond milk.

"Hey, Lauren, I'm so glad to see you back. This place isn't the same without you here." It was Judy dressed in navy slacks, a white blouse, and navy cardigan. A silver cable necklace that was a David Yurman knock-off sparkled at her throat. She walked across the room and hugged Lauren.

"Well, I'm not sure I'm really all here yet," Lauren said, "but I guess I'm better off getting my mind on work instead of..."

"I agree. Thanks for leaving me a message on my phone that you were coming in today. Have your folks left yet?" Judy put her brown lunch bag in the refrigerator.

"No, they leave this afternoon. I'll be taking them to the airport so I have to leave here at three. Michael's parents already left."

"And how are they coping?"

"Just as you would expect. They had their moments. Mom Casey was taking tranquilizers so that helped her through the week. And Dad Casey ... well ... men are better at hiding their feelings. We had some real heart-to-heart talks. Mom Casey told me she felt close to me, like the daughter she never had. That meant a lot to me to hear that. How many mothers-in-law say something like that? She also told me that I shouldn't blame myself, which of course I do. She wants us to keep up our relationship, and said we should continue our Sunday phone calls. She said it would be too much to not only lose her son, but to lose me, too. I hadn't even looked at it that way. I feel close to Michael's parents so her words were a comfort."

Judy glanced at her watch. "Let's talk later. What do you say if I come over tonight and we have dinner? Maybe order Chinese? My treat."

"You're not going to the gym after work?

"No, my body needs a break. I'm sore from doing crunches."

"I could use your company. Will you leave here the usual time, five-thirty?"

"If I don't, I'll call you. Otherwise, I'll be at your house about six-fifteen."

"So where were you?" Lauren glanced at Judy with a conspiratorial look.

"Huh? What are you talking about?"

"Did you have a date? You weren't home when I called last night."

Judy didn't say a word. Her smile was enough of an answer. Lauren was glad if Judy had had a date. Divorced for two years, she lacked confidence in herself until she found out from a mutual friend the real reason her husband neglected her in the bedroom. He was a closeted homosexual. With that knowledge, she could reevaluate her life and had a professional makeover. The session did wonders for her self-esteem. Now she was slimming down and toning her body. She also went shopping for a new wardrobe, asking Lauren to come along and help her. Judy went from looking like an aging college student in jeans and tee shirts to a professional woman in business attire.

"Well, I want to hear all about it tonight. I've got to see Liz now." Lauren turned and headed down the hallway to Liz's office. Magazine and newspaper ads the agency produced for their clients hung on the walls in gleaming chrome frames.

Liz's office space was small since she shared it with an intern. Stacks of papers were all over Liz's desk. Under it were stacks of advertising trade journals. There was a bookcase filled with three-ring binders that held purchase orders and talent release contracts. In one corner was a potted dieffenbachia that was badly in need of water. It irritated Lauren that people neglected their plants. She thought it a crime, really. *Why bother having them if you're not going to take care of them?*

"Hi, Lauren. Sit down." Liz cleared off the one visitor's chair next to her desk and deposited the file folders on the floor under her desk.

Lauren took a seat and sipped her coffee.

"What you've been through! I'm so sorry. You made such a beautiful couple. It's such a tragedy. Do the police have any leads?" Liz rambled.

"Please, Liz. If you don't mind. I know you mean well, but I ... I ... don't want to get into it. It's hard for me to talk about it." Lauren shifted in the chair.

"I'm sorry. Me and my big mouth," Liz said. She looked down in shame like a child who was just scolded.

"It's all right." Lauren touched her arm with reassurance. "Listen, I came to talk to you about the production schedule for Mirabella."

Liz looked up. "Well, I hope you don't need anything done soon because I'm tied up with the new television campaign for the cruise line."

"So all the spots finally got approved for Royal Fiesta?"

Liz nodded yes. "Now I've got to line up a film production house to start filming, secure the models, and arrange for a voice-over talent."

"Well then, don't worry about Mirabella. It's not a major production. I'm just going to use some slides and some artist's renderings of the new project and have it put on a DVD, maybe use some of their special computer effects. I can handle that. I'll need to book the voice over talent and supervise him. I'll get that done first, then take it to the post production studio and finish the job of laying the voice over and music down. So don't worry about Mirabella."

"Thanks, Lauren. I appreciate it. You really are an amazing woman. I don't know how you do it," Liz said.

Lauren got up from the chair, feeling patronized. "All right. I'll send you an email with a timeline when I have it settled, okay?"

"Great, Lauren. Thanks again."

Lauren left Liz's cubicle feeling confident that producing the video would go smoothly. All she needed now was the complete file on Mirabella. She stopped at Bill Parson's office. He was on the telephone, but he motioned to her to take one of seats in front of his desk. She thought he was a handsome man, in his early forties, with dark wavy hair and hazel eyes. By Lauren's guess, he was six feet tall and had the body of a swimmer, broad shoulders and trim waist. He wore impeccably tailored suits every workday, except Friday which was dress-down day. Then he'd show up wearing designer jeans and an open-collared shirt or a polo shirt. Even then he looked like he could model for *GQ*.

There was a credenza behind his desk which displayed the obligatory family photos of his wife and two adorable children, a six-year-old son and an eight-year-old daughter. Lauren remembered that Bill had told her that his wife had been his high school sweetheart and that her health was fragile. Since she was an epileptic on medication, she wasn't allowed to drive. She was very dependent on Bill and apparently he didn't mind. Lauren looked with amusement at a Mickey Mouse gum ball machine and remote-control airplane that looked like one Bill probably owned as a kid. The account executive's desk was a complete contrast to Liz's. Except for his computer and desk accessories, his desk was clear except for the phone, a notepad, a pen and a file folder. He smiled at her as he continued talking and raised his eyes upward as if was bored with the person on the phone. He looked back at her and stared directly into Lauren's eyes, making her feel uncomfortable. Although Bill was married, he was always flirtatious around Lauren. She believed it would only take a little encouragement on her part for things to go further.

Finally, Bill hung up the phone. "Sorry that took so long, Lauren. And by the way, my condolences again. I didn't really get to talk to you for more than a minute at the funeral and I wasn't able to make it to your home afterward."

"I understand. I came by since I want to get started on the presentation. Can you give me everything you have on Mirabella? If you have any thoughts that I should keep in mind in writing about the new project, I'd appreciate it."

"You know who the audience is -- the Miami City Commission. And since we have "Florida in the Sunshine Law," the public and press are always invited to attend.

Mirabella is trying to convince the board that this is a viable project. However, Mirabella is seeking to get some zoning restriction changed. This presentation is to lay the ground work to convince them of it. Your job is to first build the credibility of the company. You know, how long the company's been in business and past successful projects and then give an overview of the project. The architect for the project is Ellis Sak. He's big time as far as architects go, although I think he's on the pompous side."

"Why does Mirabella need the zoning changed?" Lauren toyed with the heart pendant hanging from the gold chain around her neck.

"This project is kind of a mixed bag. Sak's concept is a Mediterranean village so there are villas and townhouses, but here's the catch. He envisions retail shops and restaurants along the waterfront and on the second level, apartments."

"What? I can't imagine anyone wanting to live over a store or a restaurant."

"Lauren, people in Manhattan do it all the time and so do Europeans. I suppose that's who this is appealing to. Buyers gets this beautiful apartment with a fabulous view of Biscayne Bay and the convenience of having everything they need within walking distance."

"Sounds good when you say it like that, but I have my reservations. I mean, if you're living over a restaurant, won't you have all these cooking smells wafting into your apartment?"

Bill shrugged his shoulders. "I wouldn't know about that. Just don't let your reservations come through in your script. If this project gets the go-ahead, we'll be producing a 36-page brochure with floor plan inserts, ads that will run in the *New York Times,* and *Wall St. Journal,* and a DVD that can be mailed out to prospects. Plus we'll also place ads in the real estate section and run TV spots. And I almost forgot, we need to build a website. We're thinking of putting a sales pitch on that site, too. So it's a sizable account."

"I had no idea there was that much work planned. All right. Do you have the artist's renderings and the brochures from the other Mirabella projects? I'm going to need some visuals for this thing."

Bill got up from his chair and got a three-ring binder from his bookcase. It held acetate envelopes holding collateral pieces. "Here are the brochures. I'll have someone from the art department bring the renderings to your office. They were scanning them into the computer so they can use them in the ads and brochure."

Lauren stood up and took the binder from Bill. "Who's your contact at Mirabella, Bill?

"What's the matter, Lauren? Don't you read the conference reports?" Bill asked with a touch of annoyance in his voice.

"Not unless I have to. I find them boring as hell. Besides, the only reason you write them is to cover your ass," Lauren said, trying not to sound defensive.

"Well, they have saved me a couple of times," Bill admitted with a laugh.

"So, do I have to read the conference report to find out?" Lauren asked.

"I'm sorry. I usually deal with Craig Richards, but he's been out of the office. Seems he's been called away on some family emergency. I've been working with his assistant, Barbara Whitehead."

"I see. You don't mind if I call her directly do you, if I have a question or need some information?"

"Not at all, Lauren. I just thought you creatives wanted as little to do with clients as possible."

"That's true. But sometimes it's the only practical thing to do," Lauren turned to the door. "I've got my work cut out for me. Thank you for your time, Bill."

"Don't mention it." Bill gave her his best smile.

Just as Lauren arrived at her office, she was met by Eddie Gonzalez, the print production manager. He was a short, stocky man who emigrated from San Juan, Puerto Rico when he was a teenager. He had brown eyes, a broad nose, a *cafe au lait* complexion, and brown kinky hair that he kept closely cropped. Lauren thought he was one of the better production managers she had ever met. He was thorough in getting the best prices for printing and paper and was a stickler for quality. He also was a charmer when it came to women. He was holding a cardboard tube which evidently held the artists' renderings of the new project. She felt his eyes give her the head-to-toe once over.

"Now that's what I call service. I assume you have the renderings for me?

"You got it." Eddie flashed a winning smile.

Preoccupied with the work at hand, Lauren did not return the smile but simply took the tube from his hands and walked to her desk. "Thanks, Eddie. I'll bring them back when I'm finished with them."

"What are you planning to do with them?" Eddie followed her.

"I need them for a video presentation. The studio will scan them into their computer program and then we'll do some special effects."

"Well, in that case, let me get them mounted for you so they'll lie flat," Eddie suggested.

"Now why didn't I think of that?" Lauren handed the tube back to Eddie.

"Because you have an awful lot on your mind. How soon do you need them? Tomorrow okay?"

Lauren put the three-ring binder on her desk and sat down. "That's fine, Eddie. I appreciate it. Now if you'll excuse me, I've got tons to do."

Lauren turned on her computer and when she looked back at Eddie, she saw him walking out the door.

I hope he didn't think I was rude, Lauren thought. He really is a sweetheart. After closing her office door, she picked up her phone, dialed nine and entered Craig Richard's number. She left a message on his voice mail. Five minutes later, her phone rang.

"This is Lauren Casey speaking," Lauren said in her business voice.

"It's Craig Richards. You called?"

"Yes, I met with Bill Parsons this morning who gave me what he had on Mirabella, but I'm going to need some damning evidence if this plan is going to work. We need to figure out how to get it. Any thoughts right now?"

"I'm just not sure. Give me some time. Should I call you later this afternoon?"

"No, I'm leaving at three to take my parents to the airport. Why don't you come over later tonight, say seven? Then I can give you the keys to my cousin's apartment in Naples."

"All right. Your cousin agreed?"

"Actually, I haven't been able to reach her. I left voice mail messages for her. I'll call her at work again when I hang up with you."

"Good, I'll see you later."

"Don't you need my address and directions?" Lauren asked.

"No. I looked it up. That's how I called you. You've got a listed number."

"Oh, you're right. I'm not thinking," Lauren paused. She wondered if having a listed number was such a good idea now that she was living alone. "I'll see you tonight."

After she hung up with Craig, Lauren dialed her cousin Carolyn's work number. She got her voice mail again and left a detailed message that she'd like a friend to use her condo in Naples if it was available. *Where the heck could she be?* Lauren wondered.

Chapter 14

The moment Lauren walked into her house, her heart raced. She was alone in a quiet house, and she missed her parents tremendously. The goodbyes at the airport were tearful. During the drive home from the airport, Lauren fantasized about moving to New Jersey to be closer to them. She felt like an abandoned child and she longed to be on a plane heading north.

She put her purse and tote bag on the chair in the family room and went to her bedroom to change out of her black dress and pumps for jeans, a blue cotton knit top, and sandals. After she hung up her dress, she looked at Michael's clothing hanging on his side of the closet. Dress shirts, slacks, sport coats, suits, and ties were all in order. On the floor were his shoes, all arranged in a neat row. His collection of caps and hats lined the upper shelf: A Greek fishing cap. A pith helmet. A driving cap. A fedora. A Miami Dolphins cap. Everything had its place. She wondered what she should do with them, and if she could face giving them away just yet. She looked at the two storage boxes on the shelf that were labeled "ties." Just two weeks ago, Michael had gathered all his ties that were out of style, because they were too wide and asked Lauren to store them for him. She remembered asking him if he thought they'd come back in style again. His response was, "You can bet on it."

One by one, Lauren fingered the sleeve of each jacket. Then she did the same to the shirts. She put her face to the shirt he had worn out to dinner Saturday night and inhaled deeply. She could smell the faint fragrance of Pure XS.

"Oh, Michael," Lauren whispered, fighting back the tears. *"This is so unfair. How I wish Sunday never happened. How can I live without you?"*

Lauren took in a deep breath and blinked back the tears. She went to their bed and laid down, staring at the ceiling. The nightmare of the Sunday bike ride through the Grove replayed in her mind. Then her imagination took over for the parts that she did not witness. Someone drawing a gun. A shot. Michael sprawled out on the ground. The thought of it all made Lauren angry. She forced the horrible image from her mind and thought about Ted Bomar. She had never met the man, yet she hated him. She got up from the bed and went to the family room. The lights had already been turned on by the automatic timer. She pulled the Mirabella file folder from her tote bag along with a legal pad and pen. She sat in the lotus position on the couch and began writing an outline for the video presentation. She had spent the remainder of her day in the office reviewing the history of Mirabella and the housing projects that were completed, so it took Lauren just a few minutes to settle on the approach she would take.

The doorbell rang. Lauren put her work plan on the coffee table. She glanced at her watch. Judy was right on time. Lauren went to the front door and looked through the peep hole. It was dark outside and Judy was illuminated by the porch light. Lauren opened the door. "You're right on time. Come in."

Judy hugged her friend hello. "I was lucky. No accidents tonight to slow traffic down." She sniffed the air. "Something smells good."

"My mom made a pot of *pasta e fagioli* while I was at work. I thought we'd have that with a salad and bread for dinner tonight. Maybe a glass of *vino*. Instead of Chinese take-out."

"Sounds good to me." She held her friend at arm's length. "So how are you? Really?"

Lauren shrugged her shoulders.

"Your Mom and Dad leave on time?" Judy asked, purposely changing the subject when she saw Lauren's eyes glisten.

"Yes. It was hard to say goodbye. They didn't really want to leave."

"Then why didn't you have them stay longer?" Judy walked to the tub chair adjacent to the couch and plopped down. "I know you get along great with your folks."

Lauren followed her and parked herself on the couch. "No, that's not it. It's just that..."

"It's just what?"

"Nothing. I have work."

"So. You go to work. You come home. Mom and Dad are here. Your Mom would cook dinner. What's wrong with that?"

Lauren looked away. "It's not that simple."

"Sure it is," said Judy. She leaned forward and looked hard at Lauren. She hesitated and said, "Is there something you want to tell me?"

"Like what?"

"I don't know, Lauren. You're talking to me but not saying anything. I'm not a mind reader, but there's a reason you don't want your parents here. So what is it? Tell me."

Lauren got up from the couch and headed for the kitchen. "I could use a drink. Want one?"

Judy got up and followed her. "Is the Pope Catholic? Does a bear ...?"

"OKAY.!" Lauren looked at Judy and forced a smile. She got two glasses from the cabinet and went to the freezer for ice cubes.

Judy leaned against the counter. "You can't distract me with a drink. I want to know what this is all about."

Lauren took the bottle of scotch and sparkling mineral water from the cabinet for herself. "Do you want Seagram's or wine?"

"Seagram's and soda. Or water. Doesn't matter. Out with it, Lauren. Quit changing the subject."

Lauren poured the drinks and gave Judy hers. "I just don't want you to over react."

"Over react to what?" The two friends raised their glasses in a silent toast and drank.

"Let me check the heat on this soup, and then let's go back to the family room and sit down. Then I'll tell you."

Lauren lifted the lid on the pot and gave the soup a stir. On the way to the family room, Lauren closed the vertical blinds to the sliding glass doors to the patio. "Sometimes I feel like I'm in fishbowl with all the glass in this house."

"You better make sure to keep them closed at night, especially since you're alone. You never know if some rapist is on the loose."

"Well, there's a nice thought. Thank you very much."

"I'm sorry. I'm being me—flip. I didn't think. I don't want to scare you, but you're alone and you need to be careful." Judy sat down and then said. "Okay, I'm sitting. Now tell me."

Lauren trusted Judy but wasn't sure if she would get the support she wanted from her. She sat down and was silent.

Judy stared at Lauren. "Well? I'm all ears! Out with it!"

Lauren took a long swallow of her drink and looked directly at Judy. "I'm going to nail the bastard that killed Michael."

"Right. And I'm going to win the $17 million Florida lottery on Saturday."

"Look. I'm serious. I have a plan."

"Well, I say forget it. Leave that stuff to the police."

"The police? What's one more dead body? One more unsolved murder? You know how many people get murdered in Miami? Hundreds! How many do you think they solve? The clearance rate is extremely low. They have more cases than they can really handle. Have you ever heard of the Cold Case Squad? These are detectives assigned to homicides that remained unsolved year after year. Their website counts twenty-five hundred cold cases. Do you think I've heard anything from the detective about Michael's case? *Nada!* Zilch! Nothing. They tell you nothing. They don't want you to learn anything. And don't forget, they always look to family members as the usual suspect. No, I'm not waiting for the police on this thing. Besides, I know who killed Michael."

Judy coughed on her drink. "What did you say? You know who killed him?"

"Yes."

"Well, don't keep me in suspense! Who is it?"

"Ted Bomar."

"Ted Bomar? Who the hell is he?"

"He's the CEO of Mirabella."

"Mirabella? You mean Mirabella, the real estate account at the agency?"

Lauren shook her head. "You got it."

"Holy shit. I don't believe it. Where did you get that idea? That sounds totally crazy."

"I know. It's real close to home, isn't it? It's going to make my job easier."

"Wait a minute. Back up a minute. Why would Bomar want to kill Michael?"

"He thought he was Craig Richards."

"What do you mean he *thought* he was Craig Richards? And who is Craig Richards?"

"Michael is ... err ... was ... a dead ringer for Craig Richards. They look so much alike, it's scary. As for your second question—and I thought I was the only one who doesn't read status reports—he's the VP of marketing."

"This is too much. How did you put this all together? This theory of yours?"

"Craig Richards told me."

"What? Craig Richards? I can't believe what you're telling me."

"Yes, Craig Richards called me and told me. His life is in danger, right now."

Judy took another drink. "This is hard to grasp. Help me out. I don't believe a CEO would lie in wait to knock off his VP."

"He didn't do it himself! He hired someone to do it."

"You mean a hit man? A button man? A contract killer?"

Lauren shook her head yes.

"All right. So he hired someone. This is really getting good," Judy said with sarcasm coating every word. "What's the motive?"

Lauren went into detail about the toxic site and Bomar's plan to con the Broward County School Board. When she finished telling Judy the story, she noticed a change in her friend's attitude.

"This sounds incredible," Judy said. "Do you believe this Craig Richards?"

"Yes, I do."

"I don't know, Lauren. I'd be leery. What's your plan? "

"You know that video presentation that I have to write? I'm going to show Ted Bomar for who he really is. The presentation is for the Miami City Commission so I can count on the press being there. It's perfect. I'll expose the son-of-a-bitch for what he really is—a damn murderer!"

"I'm not convinced you can pull it off. You just can't accuse the guy. I mean you can, but if you want this guy to go to jail you've got to make sure you have evidence. You've got to link Bomar to whoever the hit man is." Judy let out a deep sigh. "I don't know about this. I think you're foolish."

"Judy, it will work. Craig Richards is coming here tonight to help me with the evidence." Lauren glanced at her watch. "In fact, he should be here any minute. I told him to come over at seven."

"Why didn't you tell me he was coming?"

"I just did."

Judy glared at Lauren. "I don't like it one bit. You're putting yourself in jeopardy. The whole scheme stinks."

"Judy, Michael's dead. That stinks."

Lauren was prepared for an argument, but Judy simply took a sip of her drink.

The phone rang. "That reminds me, I never did check my answering machine since I got home."

Lauren went to the kitchen and picked the phone up on the third ring. "Hello."

"Lauren, it's Detective Dolan. I called you at your office earlier, but I got your voice mail, so I thought I'd try you at home."

"I left early to take my folks to the airport," Lauren said, then realizing she didn't need to let him know where she was.

"The results from your polygraph test came back and I'm afraid it's inconclusive. I'd like you to come in and take another test. Can you come in this week?"

Lauren's stomach tightened. "Inconclusive? You want me to take another test? I don't understand what for. You don't think I had something to do with Michael's death?"

The detective's tone was impersonal and businesslike. "This is routine. Can you come in?"

"I've got a real busy week ahead at work. I was out all last week. I'm going to have to check with what I've got scheduled at the office. Can I call you and let you know when?" Lauren asked, hoping the detective didn't think she was trying to stall him even though she was.

"That's fine. Call me and let me know when you'll be in."

"I'll do that." Lauren hung up the phone and stood there, letting the detective's request sink in. She walked slowly back to the family room.

"What's the matter with you, Lauren?" Judy asked. "You look pale."

"He wants me to come in to take another polygraph," Lauren said. She eased herself onto the couch.

"You were talking to the detective?" Lauren nodded her head.

"Why does he want you to take another test?"

"He said it was inconclusive."

"Well, you're the wordsmith. You should know what that means."

"Yeah, that it doesn't tell them one way or another if I'm telling the truth. It still makes me nervous. That's all I need now on top of everything is to have the police suspect me."

"Lauren, you have nothing to worry about. You didn't do it. Don't bother going back for another polygraph. I heard it's a routine that detectives use to intimidate someone of interest to see if they can force a confession. So you should relax and don't think about it."

Lauren rubbed her temples, feeling a headache coming on. "That's easy for you to say. Well, I know a polygraph is strictly voluntary. I may just take your advice and forget about going back for another one. I don't have to, you know. Voluntary means they can't force me."

"Right. Whatever. I'm getting hungry. When are we going to eat?"

It amazed Lauren that Judy could think of food at a time like this. "Soon. I thought we'd wait until Craig gets here. Let me get some pretzels out for you," Lauren said, getting up and walking to the kitchen. She returned with the snack. "Here, this should hold you for a little while longer."

The doorbell rang and Lauren flinched.

"Take it easy, Lauren. I guess that's your guest."

Lauren looked through the peephole as usual before opening the door. "Come in, Craig. I'd like you to meet my friend Judy."

Lauren saw the uncertainty in Craig's eyes as he looked at Judy. "Lauren, I didn't know..."

"I'm sorry. I should have told you. I've been so distracted. I hope you don't mind."

"Considering the circumstances, I do," Craig said evenly.

"You can trust her. She's my best friend. Come on in," Lauren said, turning and hoping Craig would follow. "Sit down. Can I get you a drink before I serve dinner?"

Craig hesitated and then followed Lauren into the family room. "Do you have scotch?"

"Yes. On the rocks?"

"Yes, please," Craig said. He sat down on the love seat and looked at Lauren's friend. Judy's mouth dropped open and stared wide-eyed at Craig.

"Judy, this is Craig Richards," Lauren said, heading back into the kitchen to prepare the drink. "I'll just be a moment.

Craig leaned forward in his seat. "Incredible, isn't it Judy?"

"I can't believe it. Lauren filled me in before you got here. What a horrible thing. I'm sorry for staring, but I can't get over the resemblance."

"I know."

Judy hesitated and said, "Lauren told me about your plan. I think it's dangerous."

"I don't have any choice. I can't go home because Bomar has unfinished business with me. And Lauren wants to see him go to prison as much as I do."

Lauren returned and handed Craig his drink and a cocktail napkin. "Here you are."

"Thanks, Lauren," Craig said. He sipped the drink and put it on the end table next to the love seat. "Your friend isn't convinced about our plan."

Lauren looked at Judy and thought that the only way to get her support would be to plead her case. "Judy, we've been friends a long time. You know I think of you as the sister I never had. I'm here for you. I need you to be here for me now. In a matter of days this whole thing will be wrapped up and Bomar will be history. Please, Judy. Stick with me on this, please?"

Judy looked at Lauren, then at Craig and back to Lauren again. She exhaled loudly and said, "All right. I'll keep my mouth shut about this and go along with it. And if you need my help, just holler. Okay?"

"Okay, I just might need to do that. Now, if it's all right with you two, soup's on."

Judy popped up from her seat. "Finally. I'm famished."

"Did you say soup?" Craig asked.

"I hope you like *pasta e fagioli*, it's an Italian white bean and pasta soup. My Mom made it before she left today."

"I sure do. It's a favorite of mine."

"Then let's go into the dining room and sit down. I'll put the salad and bread out." Lauren rushed past them, remembering she hadn't even set the table. She grabbed teal linen placemats and napkins from the kitchen drawer, and then set the table, putting a wineglass at each place.

"I've never seen you move so fast, Lauren," Judy teased.

"I don't know about my mind lately. I can't seem to remember the little things."

"Let me help you get the salad out while you serve the soup," Judy offered. She opened the refrigerator and found the salad bowl of fresh greens. "Did you Mom make this, too?"

"Yes," Lauren sighed. "You know that I'm glad you're here tonight, but I'm not looking forward to tomorrow. It will be the first day in a very long time that I'm completely alone."

"Remember, Lauren, I'm just a phone call away."

Lauren smiled at her friend. She was grateful to have a friend like Judy. "I know that. Come on. Let's eat."

Chapter 15

When Lauren returned to the family room after saying goodnight to Judy, she found Craig sitting on the couch reading her Mirabella work plan.

"What do you think?" Lauren asked, nodding her head indicating the folder he held in his hands. She settled into the love seat

"I hope you don't mind that I took a look at it."

"No, not really. I mean, that's why we're here, isn't it?

Craig smiled. "I like your friend. She really speaks her mind."

"Yeah, that's why I like her, too. There's no BS with Judy."

"Getting back to the business at hand, I think the way you've outlined the presentation is fine. You ease into it, explaining how Bomar has built his business, citing different examples of communities and commercial projects and the obstacles he overcame to see them constructed. You get into how he wants zoning changed so he can build his Mediterranean village. Finally, whamo. You get into the deception about the toxic site, and then Bomar's plan to murder me backfired resulting in your husband's murder. That's all fine. But we should have two files to offer as evidence: the file on the toxic site and the letter of proposal that was sent to the school board."

Lauren leaned forward in her chair. "Good. Do you have them?"

"I wish I did. They're probably in Bomar's private office files under lock and key."

"Oh, great. How am I supposed to get them? Go and ask him for them?"

Craig gave her a look that told her sarcasm wasn't appreciated.

Lauren apologized. "Sorry. Since all this has happened, I find myself not acting at all like me. It's weird."

Craig nodded, acknowledging her apology was accepted. "You could call Barbara Whitehead, my assistant, and ask her for Bomar's photo that he uses for press releases. Tell her you're going to use it in the presentation. He keeps that in his file cabinet. Make an appointment for Wednesday morning. Bomar is on the golf course then and his secretary is at the nail salon. Once you follow Barbara into his office and she unlocks the cabinet, do something to get her to leave. Then you can pull the files."

"Like do what to get her to leave?"

"Good question." Craig shrugged his shoulders. "Have her paged for a phone call?"

"No, she could simply pick up the call in Bomar's office."

"That's right."

They both sat silent, each deep in thought. Finally Lauren said, "Maybe I could have something delivered that she needs to sign for."

"Nah, that's not the office routine. All deliveries are signed for by the receptionist."

Lauren sat back with a sigh. "Then I don't know. Can I get in there after hours when no one's around?"

"I suppose you could." Craig fished the key ring out of his pocket and removed a key. "Here's the key to the office."

"Then what about the key to Bomar's file cabinet?"

"Damn! You could try his secretary's desk drawer providing she doesn't lock it before she leaves for the day. If that fails, you can try picking the lock."

"This is getting very complicated," Lauren muttered.

"You're not going to back out of this, are you?" Craig's eyes searched Lauren's for reassurance.

Lauren glanced away. "No. I'm going to have to psyche myself up for this. Breaking and entering isn't something that comes naturally to me."

Craig rolled his eyes. "Well, remember why you're doing this."

"I know."

"Get this presentation done and the rest will take care of itself."

"Easy for you to say." Lauren rose from the loveseat. "I never did check my answering machine. Excuse me a minute."

Lauren walked into her office and hit the play button on her answering machine.

"Lauren, it's Carolyn. I'm sorry I haven't gotten back to you sooner, but I was away on a business trip. I'm getting ready to fly out again tonight for another trip. About the condo in Naples. Go right ahead and use it. My tenant already left to go back home to Ohio. I'll call the resident manager to let him know someone will be staying at my place, otherwise he'd call the police. You have a spare key, if I remember correctly. Just tell your friend to be careful about my white carpet, okay? Maybe he can take his shoes off and leave them on the lanai by the door. Is that weird of me? Well, I've got to run. I'll call you soon, Cuz, just as soon as I get back—probably in a week or so. I hope you're well. Give my love to your gorgeous husband."

Lauren realized that her cousin didn't know about Michael. It would have to wait until she could speak to Carolyn on the phone.

When Lauren returned to the family room, Craig was gone. She saw the sliding glass door to the patio was open and found him there in the darkness. She remembered it was the first place she always looked when she couldn't find Michael elsewhere in the house. He loved being out there where he could admire all his plants. "There you are. I thought maybe you took off without saying goodbye."

"No, that's not my style. It's nice out here. I have a screened-in pool and patio at home, too, and I really enjoy it. It's so peaceful."

Lauren joined him at the patio table and sat down. "Yes, it is. I spend a lot of time out here, too. I find the pool so relaxing."

She studied Craig's face and wished that he was really Michael. She admired his strong jaw line and his straight nose. She remembered she once remarked to Michael that his nose reminded her of the noses on Roman statues. Or even Michelangelo's *David*. Michael had kidded her that he had a Roman nose all right—a nose that roamed all over his face. He had made her laugh. And now it was hard to look at Craig and not yearn for Michael.

"There was a message from my cousin Carolyn. You can stay at her condo in Naples. She said to be careful of the white carpet. So that means taking your shoes off at the door. The manager is very strict there so make sure you park your car in the covered space with her unit number—three-ten. Otherwise your car will be towed." She noticed Craig raised his eyebrows.

"Before you leave, I'll get my folder out for her place. It has the key, directions, an area map, and a tourist guide for places to go including restaurants and supermarkets."

"My, are you always so organized?"

Lauren tried to smile. "I'm afraid so."

Craig cleared his throat. "There's one other thing we haven't figured out."

"What's that?"

"Who the contract killer is."

"Do you still think your house is being watched?" Lauren's eyes widened at the thought.

"Ah, I see what you're getting at. You think Bomar's hired gun might be waiting for me at my house. It's possible. I just don't know if he'd still have someone out there after a week."

"You want to find out?"

"Sure, but I don't want to take the chance. If I go back there, I could get killed."

"Well, I could go."

Craig's face showed surprise. "Hmm. Okay, suppose you go. How are you going to get an I.D. on the guy?"

"The license plate on his car. I'll call the Department of Motor Vehicles in Tallahassee."

"I don't think they will give you the information.

"That's probably right. But if at least we had the tag and description of the dirt bag, that would help."

"Of course, a cop could get it for you in a heartbeat."

"No thanks, I don't feel like asking any cops for a favor. I think I should go now to see if anyone is surveilling your house."

Craig dictated the address while Lauren entered it into the map app on her smart phone.

"Thanks," said Lauren. "That's a nice neighborhood."

"You'll see the house number on the mail box at the curb. Do you have a flashlight in your car?"

"Yes."

"The street isn't lighted very well so you may need to use it."

Lauren looked the map. "All right, I'm on my way. Make yourself comfortable. Turn on the TV, if you like."

Lauren grabbed her purse and left.

The drive from Kendall to Coconut Grove was uneventful with Lauren only having to stop for three traffic lights along Dixie Highway. She found herself tightly gripping the steering wheel worrying about encountering the hit man. She wondered what she would say if someone stopped her. *But why would someone stop me?* Lauren thought. *This isn't a gated community. If somebody does ask me, I could say I was looking for a house and give another street name. Yes, that's what I'll say. That's innocent enough.*

Lauren had no trouble finding the street, thanks to her phone's GPS. He was right about the street. Street lights were few and far between, but all of the homes had exterior landscape lighting and porch lights that illuminated each luxurious estate. Lauren wondered how much Craig made a year to be able to afford a home in such an upscale neighborhood. She figured he had to have paid at least a million dollars or more for the place.

Lauren opened the glove box, reached for the flashlight, and turned it on. She shined the light on the mail boxes on her left and found Craig's house. At the curb was his mail box. She noticed that the door was open because the box was crammed with mail. Obviously Craig hadn't called the post office to stop delivery. Lauren looked up and down the street. No cars were parked on the street. She noticed some cars parked in driveways but other than that, Lauren didn't see a car that she'd consider a surveillance vehicle. She pulled into Craig's driveway and shined the flashlight scanning the front of the house. Everything looked normal to her. There was even a light on inside. Lauren guessed Craig had his lights on an automatic timer like she did. She got out of her car and went to the mail box. She pulled a large bundle from the box and then shined the light inside to see if any mail remained. There were a bunch of envelopes which had been pushed to the back of the box. Lauren retrieved them, closed the mail box and returned her car. She laid the bundle on the passenger seat and out of curiosity, flipped through the mail. She found nothing out of the ordinary, just bills, advertising circulars, catalogs from department stores, and a travel magazine. She looked up and down the street once more before putting her car into reverse. *So much for identifying the hit man*, Lauren thought as she drove back home. *I got all worked up over nothing.*

When Lauren walked back into the house, she found Craig watching an old movie.

"What do you have there?" Craig asked. There was a look of shock on his face as he stared at the bundle of mail in Lauren's arms.

"Your mail. It was bulging out of the box," Lauren explained. She wasn't prepared for Craig's reaction, and she swallowed hard.

Craig's yelled, "Don't you realize how dangerous that was?"

"What? I just got your mail. I thought I was doing you a favor."

"Lauren, don't you see? If anyone saw you get my mail, he would figure you know where I am in order to give it to me. Now your life could be in jeopardy, too."

"But there wasn't anybody around to see me get it. I checked. Honestly. There wasn't a sole person on the street, nor a car for that matter. There were only cars parked in the driveways." Lauren walked to the cocktail table by the couch and put the mail down in front of Craig. "If I did something wrong, I'm sorry."

Craig shook his head. "I'm sorry for yelling. So you didn't see anything usual?"

"I'm afraid not. Do you have an automatic timer turn on your lights?"

Craig flipped through his mail. "Yes. I assume the lights were on."

"Yes." Lauren collapsed on the love seat. She felt very foolish for not thinking about her actions. Now she began to feel paranoid and wondered if, in fact, someone did see her. She hadn't noticed if she had been followed. "Do you think someone saw me?"

"I don't know. I wasn't there," Craig said, clearly annoyed with her.

They both sat quietly watching TV for a few minutes. Craig was the first to break the silence. "If I over reacted, I'm sorry."

"And I'm sorry for not thinking," Lauren said avoiding eye contact.

"Okay. Do you still want to go to Bomar's office?"

"Yes, but I think I've had enough excitement for one night."

"I'm not suggesting tonight."

Lauren looked Craig in the eyes. "Sorry. I guess tomorrow night. Does Bomar work late on Tuesday?"

"Probably not past six or seven. Depending if he has a date or not."

"A date? I assumed he's married."

Craig looked at her like how can she be so naive. "He is, but that doesn't stop him."

"I don't know how his wife could put up with it."

"You're assuming she knows."

"Craig, believe me. A woman knows when her husband is not faithful. Trust me on that one."

"Are you speaking from experience?"

"Not with Michael. No. I know he's been faithful to me since we were married. But I knew in prior relationships when my boyfriend was seeing someone else on the side."

"But that's different, isn't it? That's not marriage. Well, never mind about that. It's getting late and I should be going. Can I have the key to the condo?"

Lauren hesitated, then said, "It's awfully late to start driving to Naples. Why don't you wait till the morning? You can sleep in the guest room."

Craig wrinkled his forehead. "You think it's such a good idea, me staying here?"

Lauren chewed on a fingernail. "It's probably not a good idea, but I'd feel better if you stayed tonight. I'm feeling a little nervous about this mail thing. What if I was followed?"

"Does this house have an alarm system?"

"Yes."

"Then don't forget to set it."

"I'll do it now."

"But first, I need to get my things out of the trunk of my car," Craig said. He got up and let himself out through the front door.

Lauren followed him and looked up and down her street for a suspicious car. She saw none. She took a deep breath and let it out slowly. She felt uneasy. She knew it was stupid to have a stranger staying in her house, but she had to trust Craig. She just didn't want to spend the night alone in her house. At least not tonight.

Craig approached her carrying a nylon sports bag. "I travel light."

"I can see that. If you need anything, let me know. Let me show you to your room. But first things first."

Lauren locked the front door and set the alarm, entering the code. She led the way down the short hallway to the guest bedroom and flipped on the light. It was elegantly furnished with a queen-size bed, a dresser with a mirror, a candlestick lamp and a powder blue Queen Anne chair. On the walls were framed watercolor florals which harmonized with the cornflower blue and pale yellow of the comforter. Two walls had windows which were covered by Roman shades in the same fabric. The effect was feminine and charming.

"I hope you'll be comfortable. I hope you don't think it's too feminine. Michael always thought so."

Craig walked into the room and put his sports bag on the chair. "It's a pretty room."

"Thank you. Are you ready to turn in?" Lauren asked.

"Not really. I thought I watch the rest of that movie."

"That sounds like a good idea. I'm still wound up. If I were to go to bed now, I just lie there staring at the ceiling."

In the family room, Lauren asked, "Before I sit down, can I get you anything?"

"Just a glass of water, thank you."

Lauren returned with two glasses of water. Craig had already made himself comfortable at the opposite end of the couch from where Lauren usually sat. She handed him a glass and settled down in her usual spot.

Lauren grabbed a pillow and wrapped her arms around it. Her eyes were fixed on the TV screen, but her mind was elsewhere. She felt distracted and unable to concentrate. From time to time, she felt Craig looking at her.

Finally, he said, "It's been years since I've watched TV with a woman. I guess it's an odd thing to say."

Lauren looked at him. "Not really. It's not something most people I know do on a date. Watching TV together is something you do together after you've known each other for a while and are comfortable."

"Yeah, I guess you're right," Craig said. "I was just thinking."

"About your wife?" Lauren asked.

"Yes, I really miss her. She was more than my wife. She was my best friend."

"I've only heard one other man say that about his wife and that's my boss. I felt that way about Michael, too. We were best friends. I think that's important in a marriage. Being friends means being there for someone, through all of it. It means sharing your life in so many ways. The good times. And the rough times. Of course, that's all over now."

Lauren felt her chest tighten and she knew she would cry if she'd didn't leave the room. "If you'll excuse me, I'm more tired than I thought. Feel free to stay up, but I'm ready to go to bed. Good night, Craig."

"Good night. I'll see you in the morning."

Lauren felt Craig's eyes on her back as she walked out of the family room toward her bedroom. *He has Michael's face. How I wish he were him. Yet I can't forget that this man is, in a way, responsible for Michael's death. And here I am helping him. But I have to. I have to put away Michael's killer. I need justice! I'll be glad to sleep and not think about this for a while,* Lauren thought. *That is, if I can fall asleep.*

Chapter 16

Lauren was relieved when her alarm went off at seven. She had awakened from a dream around four o'clock and from then on, she had tossed and turned, dozing in and out of sleep. The dream had deeply disturbed her for it had seemed so real.

In the dream, she was on the patio wearing nothing but a terry bathrobe. It was nighttime and all the lights were off in the house. She slipped the robe off and draped it over the patio chair. She dove into the pool and swam two laps. She leaned back and floated, stretching her legs out, feeling the cool water caress her skin. Suddenly she was yanked beneath the surface and she opened her eyes to see Michael pulling her to him. He kissed her on her mouth and she struggled with him to rise to the surface. Together they broke through the water and Michael held her tightly. They kissed each other passionately and Lauren told him how much she missed him. She had buried her face in his neck and she could smell his cologne. She felt intoxicated by all her senses. She looked at him to see his familiar smile. But something wasn't quite right. Somehow there had been a switch. The face was Michael's, but she realized the man was Craig. She broke free of him, screaming, and then awoke.

She laid in bed thinking about Michael and Craig. She'd tried to analyze her dream. She missed Michael beyond words. She felt empty and depressed. Just looking at Craig was a constant reminder of her loss. Could Craig replace Michael? Never. Not in a million years. After all, if it weren't for Craig, if he didn't look so much like her husband, Michael would be alive today. The thought nagged at her making her feel agitated and confused.

Lauren got out of bed, thinking about the full day of work she had ahead of her. She put on her robe over her nightgown, went to the kitchen to make coffee. After she poured herself a glass of grapefruit juice, she went down the hall to see if Craig was up. The door to the bathroom was closed and she heard the water running in the sink. Shaving, she figured. She knocked on the door and said, "Craig, I've put coffee on so help yourself to it and whatever you want to eat for breakfast. I'll be getting ready for work."

"All right, thanks."

Lauren returned the juice glass to the kitchen in exchange for coffee and took it with her to the bathroom. While showering, she thought about her agenda for the day, figuring that most of it would be spent writing the Mirabella script. She would need to have it finished by tomorrow morning so that she could get to the recording studio that afternoon and get the audio portion completed. By Thursday morning she would have to complete the video portion and then lay in the audio track. Of course, this did not leave much time for client approval, but Lauren knew she would have to plan on having two versions of the script; a phony one for agency/client approval, the other that would implicate Ted Bomar in the murder of her husband. That was easy enough to do on her computer. She just had to change the ending. She thought about Bomar, thinking how vile he must be. That was enough to give her the courage to find the files in his office after work. She just hoped she wouldn't get caught. She also decided she would try to find more background information on Bomar, other than what she already had in regard to Mirabella.

By the time she finished showering and dressing, Lauren felt like a rubber band stretched too tight. When she walked into the kitchen, she found Craig reading the newspaper and eating a bagel with cream cheese. She thought he looked particularly handsome in the most well-groomed sense of the word. He was clean shaven and his hair was still damp from his shower. She could smell the citrus fragrance of an after shave, grateful it wasn't the cologne Michael wore. He looked up from an article he was reading. "Good morning. How did you sleep or shouldn't I ask?"

"Is it that obvious I had a bad night?" As soon as the words were out, Lauren knew she sounded self-centered.

"You just look a little tired, that's all. But the dress suits you. I like blue."

"It's not blue. It's turquoise."

"Turquoise is still blue."

"No, it's not. Your shirt is blue. The dress is turquoise."

"All right already. I'm not going to start the day arguing with you. Maybe you ought to go back to bed."

"Oh, sure. Like I have time to lie around all day like you can. I've got work to do. To save your ass, I might add."

"Hold on a minute. What am I hearing from you?"

"Well, think about it. If it weren't for you, Michael wouldn't be dead. If he weren't dead, I wouldn't be standing here wondering how I am going to get everything done, plus break into your boss' office tonight. Do you realize the risk? I could get myself killed."

Craig looked at her silently for a moment and with true concern in his voice said, "Yes, I do. And I do appreciate what you're doing. I also know that I don't have any other choice. I don't think you do, either. What do you think would happen if you went to the police now?"

"You mean, tell them the story about Bomar and you?"

Craig nodded his head, "Yes. Do you think they'd believe you? Don't you think they'd think this was a story you made up?"

"I see what you're getting at." Lauren looked away from Craig's penetrating eyes. "A grieving, hysterical wife grasping at straws."

"Lauren, at this point, we need to put everything together in a tidy, convincing little package for the police. Bomar, the motive, the evidence, everything. You see, your video and Bomar's reaction to it will show everyone that Bomar is guilty of murder."

Lauren let out a deep sigh. "I sure hope so. I'm just scared. Especially after the foolish thing I did by getting your mail. I just don't know if my nerves can last through the next couple of days."

"Well, you'll be safe at work. If you don't feel safe here, you might want to stay at Judy's place."

"That's a thought. I just may do that." Lauren glanced at her watch. "If I don't leave in another few minutes, I'm going to be late for work. I've got a ton of stuff to do. Are you about ready to leave?"

"Sure, but aren't you going to have breakfast?"

"No. I'll get something at work. There's a little convenience store off the lobby where I can get a bagel or a muffin."

"All right. I'll just be a minute." Craig got up and went to the guest room while Lauren cleared his place at the table. By the time Craig returned, Lauren had rinsed off the dishes and put them in the dishwasher.

"All right. I'm ready to go."

Lauren dried her hands on a dishtowel. "Just a sec and I'll get the folder for you on Naples."

"Ah yes, the folder," Craig said, smiling at her.

Craig was waiting at the front door.

"Here's the folder. I'll call you at my cousin's condo." Lauren looked at the cell phone in his hand. "And if I don't reach you, I'll call your cell phone."

"When can I expect to hear from you?" Craig put the file folder in his sports bag.

"I'll probably call you after I visit your office tonight. That is, if I get out of there alive."

Craig rolled his eyes and sighed. "Well, good luck. Don't do anything foolish. Make sure no one is in the office before you go in. And leave everything as you found it."

He paused a moment. "You know, I do appreciate what you're doing. And I'll be anxious to hear from you."

Lauren watched Craig walk to his car and drive away. Before she closed the front door, she looked up and down the street. Catty-corner from her house, she noticed a pick-up truck from Aqua Pool parked at the curb. Lauren thought, *a pool service at the Millers? John always told me it thought it was a waste of money because it's so easy to take care of the pool himself. Maybe he's not feeling well. Or he just got a big raise.*

The first thing Lauren did when she arrived at work was to type a production schedule for the Mirabella video and email it to Liz, Bill Parsons, and Greg. She hoped that would allow her to work without interruption.

She then started writing the script. At ten o'clock, she called the *Miami News* and asked to speak to Neal Adams, the reporter who wrote the story about Michael's murder.

"This is Neal Adams."

"Neal, this is Lauren Casey. You interviewed me for the story on my husband's murder."

"Sure, I remember. How's the investigation going?"

"I haven't heard anything from the police. Listen, I was wondering if you could do me a favor. The newspaper has archives. Could you put in a request to dig up some information for me?"

"I could switch you over to library services. They can help you."

"I know that, but my request wouldn't be a priority. I really need the information right away to complete a project at work. After being out all last week, I don't have much time. In fact, I need the information today. I know they would give a request from a reporter top priority. Aren't I right?"

"You're right. What is it that you need?"

Lauren knew she had aroused his curiosity. "I'm writing a video presentation for a city commission meeting on behalf of Mirabella Corporation. They're looking for site approval on a project. I need to give a little history. What do you have on Mirabella and Ted Bomar?"

"You're talking about a big league developer. I'm sure there have been stories on him. I'll put in the request and email it to you. Give me your address."

She recited her email address and Neal repeated it back to her. "Neal, thanks a lot. If I can return the favor, let me know."

"You may already have. Who knows? You say Bomar's got a new project going? That just might make a good feature story."

"Then do me a favor. If you get a story angle, call me. After all, Mirabella is our client. Okay?"

"I'll remember to do that."

Hearing him hang up, Lauren now regretted calling Neal Adams. She didn't want some reporter snooping around. *Too late now. That's what I get for being impulsive.* She hung up the receiver and continued working on the script.

By noon, Lauren was ready to take a break for lunch. She had skipped breakfast and her stomach growled in hunger. She grabbed her purse and walked down the hall to the printer to retrieve several pages of articles on Bomar and Mirabella that Neal had emailed her. She planned to read them while she had her lunch.

Lauren left the office and took the elevator to the lobby. She stopped at The Emporium and bought a chicken Caesar salad and an iced tea to go. She decided to have her lunch on the terrace fronting the bay where there were about a dozen tables with canvas umbrellas and patio chairs. It was a sunny, breezy day in South Florida and many employees took their break out here in the warm air. She found a table farthest from the door so she could have her lunch without distraction.

Between bites of salad and sips of tea, Lauren began reading the email Neal had sent her. He advised her that he only sent real news about the company and Bomar, neglecting what the paper called "advertorials," feature stories that were paid for by the advertiser that were placed in the weekend real estate section.

When she finished reading, she realized that she didn't get what she had expected. She had hoped that she would read that Bomar was a convicted felon and that he went to jail on a real estate scam of some sort. Instead she had read the usual business news about the various Mirabella projects the company had been developing at the time the stories were written.

She remembered the first time she visited the sales center of a Mirabella development of single-family homes in the Kendall area. Since Judy and Lauren were assigned to an advertising campaign, they took a tour of the model homes and were initially impressed with them. When they returned to the sales center, Lauren raved to the sales manager how much she liked the homes; that she would even consider buying one. She was surprised when the sales manager told her she shouldn't waste her money. When she asked him why, he simply said that he has seen the way the homes are built. When Lauren countered that the homes have to pass inspection, he simply rolled his eyes. He didn't say anything more about it, but Lauren figured he meant inspectors were bribed. Lauren wondered if the sales manager still worked for Mirabella.

Lauren glanced at her watch. It was 12:35. She got up and discarded the plastic cup and salad container in the trash can. She put the pages in her leather purse and returned to the building. The lobby was busy with workers spilling out from the elevators on their way to lunch. Lauren waited for an elevator to empty so she could get on and go up to her office.

"Lauren, there you are," Judy said, the last person to step off the elevator. "I stopped by your office to see if you want to go out to lunch."

"Oh, I'm sorry, Judy," Lauren said. She stepped into the elevator and put her finger on the open door button so the elevator doors would remain open. "I already had a quick lunch on the patio. I've got to finish writing the script this afternoon so Greg can look at it before it gets sent to the client. I have a five o'clock meeting with him."

Judy frowned. "That's okay. I'm just used to having lunch with you every day.

"Well, how about if I call you later tonight?"

Judy smiled. "Actually I have a date tonight."

"Anyone I know?"

"No. it's a blind date. I'll tell you about it tomorrow."

"Maybe we'll make it lunch then, okay?"

"Fine with me," Judy said, walking toward the parking garage.

Lauren took her finger off the button and the elevator door closed. She punched the button for the seventh floor and watched the floor numbers light up over the door as the elevator ascended to her destination. Somehow having this visual to focus on while she was isolated from her world eased her fear of being closed in. She knew she wasn't alone with this phobia.

When Lauren returned to her office, her voice mail light flashed on her phone indicating she had a message. There was one from Liz who said she received the production schedule and was just reminding her to book the talent for the voice over if she hadn't already done so.

"Boy, am I losing it," muttered Lauren. "I forgot."

She first called the studio to reserve it for one o'clock Wednesday and called Marshall Taylor, the voice over talent. She was relieved that no one had a conflict with her time scheduling. She filled in the information in her appointment book so she wouldn't forget. She then dialed Greg's extension.

"Greg, it's Lauren."

"Hi. Are you ready to show me what you've got on the script?"

"I will be in a few hours. Will you be in all afternoon?"

"Yes. When you're ready, just come in and see me. How's it coming?"

"Just fine. Since I wrote an outline first, the writing is going pretty smoothly."

"Good. Then I'll see you a little later."

She felt nervous and distracted. She had a lot on her mind and it was a struggle for her to focus on her project. She took a butterscotch from the candy jar that sat on her desk and popped the treat into her mouth. She read what she had written so far and resumed writing.

By four-thirty, she had finished both versions of the script. She printed out two copies of the bogus version for Greg to review. The other version Lauren saved on a USB flash drive, which she put in her purse. She left her office to pick up the copy from the printer in the hallway. She returned to her office and stapled the pages together. It dawned on her that if Bomar went to jail because of her doing, the agency could lose the account. The thought made her very anxious because losing a major piece of business could cost some people their jobs. Including hers. She pushed the thought from her mind and gathered a clipboard, the copies of the script, and a pen.

When she reached Greg's office, she found him on the phone. He waved her in and indicated for her to sit down. Greg was very traditional in his taste in office furniture. He sat in a leather upholstered executive chair at an oak vintage roll-top desk which was up against one wall. On the floor was an Oriental carpet in rich tones of burgundy and royal blue. On the opposite wall there were framed advertising awards that agency had won over the years.

Lauren took a seat on the black leather couch which offered her a floor to ceiling view of the bay. Against another wall was a curio cabinet which displayed Greg's collection of antique toys and children's banks. She knew Greg and his wife shared a passion for collectibles after being a guest in their home for the agency's Christmas party. She was delighted with the Victrola that still played records by simply cranking the handle and she admired Greg's wife's collection of antique silver spoons.

Greg hung up the phone. "Sorry about that."

"No problem. Here's the script. Do you want me to leave it with you or stay while you look it over?"

Greg thumbed through the pages. "Unless you have something you need to take care of right now, just stay."

"On second thought, if you'll excuse me, I'll be back in a few minutes. Shall I bring back a cup of coffee for you on my way back?"

Greg glanced up from reading. "No, thanks."

The Deadly Game

When Lauren returned from the ladies room, she found Greg on the phone again. He mouthed the word "Sorry" and rolled his eyes. Lauren wondered how long he would be. She debated whether she should sit down or not. If she left, she figured Greg could be on the phone for an hour. He was a charming guy who had one amusing antidote after another to tell. She whispered to him, "Will you be on the phone much longer?"

Greg nodded no. Lauren took her seat and picked up *Florida Trend* magazine. She wished it was *Travel & Leisure,* but that's all that was on the table before her. She was tense and eager to review the script with Greg so she simply glanced at the pictures, which were in short supply considering this was a business publication.

Lauren looked at her watch and then at Greg, hoping he would get the hint to get off the phone. It worked. Greg said his goodbyes and hung up

. "I'm sorry. Guess who that was?" Greg looked amused.

"I haven't the foggiest. Who was it?" Lauren smiled and hoped her tone of voice sounded sincere.

"It was Tom." Greg sounded out "Tom" in a slow Southern drawl.

Lauren mimicked the drawl. "Tom? My word. And pray tell what is he up to?"

Tom owned a small ad agency specializing in retail accounts. He was born and raised in Atlanta and had a heavy Southern accent. However, with so many northern transplants in Miami, hardly anyone could believe the accent was genuine. New acquaintances of Tom at Ad Club functions typically were incredulous. But Lauren knew the accent was the real thing. Lauren had worked for Tom for two years on the Hoffman Jewelers account. One day the receptionist was out sick and Lauren was asked to answer the phone while the temp from the employment agency went out to lunch. When she picked up the phone, a voice that sounded exactly like Tom asked to speak to Tom. Lauren responded by saying." Tom, you're such a kidder. I know it's you."

The voice said, "This isn't Tom. It's his brother Tim."

Lauren apologized and transferred the call to Tom. Later that day, Tim came by the office and Tom showed him around and introduced him to the employees. Lauren was surprised to see that Tim was Tom's identical twin, with the same face, only Tim had graying hair. Tom had jet black hair and from then on, the employees assumed Tom dyed his hair.

Greg shook his head in amazement. "Poor guy. His creative director left, opened his own ad agency and took the Hoffman Jewelers account with him."

"Well, I don't think Tom has much to worry about. He'll probably get the account back eventually. Only Tom knows how to handle Irwin Hoffman. They go back for 15 years."

Lauren picked up her copy of the script. "Do you think we can get back to the script? If you have any changes or suggestions you'd like me to make, I'm going to have to do it tonight so we can send this thing to the client first thing in the morning for approval."

Greg frowned. Lauren knew he wanted to chit-chat. "All right. As far as time, we're behind the eight ball on this one."

Lauren bristled. "Not your fault, mind you. You couldn't control the circumstances that you were out for a whole week. I could have written it myself, but I figured it would have taken me twice as long, since I would have to familiarize myself with Mirabella. You're the expert on the account."

Lauren interrupted. "That's all right, Greg. Let's just move on. It's pretty cut and dry. I mean, the job is just to lay out the facts in a convincing way so the city commissioners will give Mirabella the approval on the zoning variances they need. I simply built a credibility story. Have far have you gotten before you got your phone call?"

"I'm on the third page. Sounds good so far." Greg resumed reading and Lauren reviewed her copy at the same time. She watched him with a tinge of annoyance as he penciled in and crossed out a few words. It was her anxiety. Normally his edits didn't affect her. Finally he handed his copy of the script to her.

"I think you did a fine job. Just a few minor suggestions." Greg smiled at her.

Lauren paged through the copy and found very few changes. It wouldn't take her but a few minutes to revise the script. She felt a little relieved this hurtle was over and she still had time to accomplish the rest of her tasks.

"Fine. Thanks for taking the time, Greg." Lauren got up from the couch and headed for the door. "I'll take care of this now and email a revised copy to for Bill so he can forward it to the client first thing tomorrow morning for approval."

"Okay, Lauren. See you in the morning. And relax. You seem nervous."

Lauren gave him a half-heartened smile and thought, *if you only knew.*

Chapter 17

Lauren sat in her car staring at the glass doors to the lobby of the Mirabella office building. It was one of the ubiquitous, mirrored-skinned buildings which were built in the early 70s that reflected the blue skies and changing cloud formations. She had found a metered parking place right in the front of the building on Alhambra Circle in the heart of Coral Gables. The digital clock on the dashboard displayed 6:40 and for the most part, the boulevard was deserted of pedestrian traffic. She debated whether to wait until seven o'clock to enter the building, thinking she'd have a better chance of going undetected.

After five minutes, she was having second thoughts about going through with her mission. She knew she better enter the building now before she lost her nerve completely. Lauren locked her car and walked to the building entrance, her high heels clicking on the tiles. Once inside, she scanned the building's directory to find Mirabella occupied the penthouse. *I shouldn't be surprised,* she thought. *A company as big as Mirabella would be in the penthouse, the top floor of the building.*

She pressed the call button for the elevator and waited for what seemed like an eternity. The elevator doors opened, Lauren stepped in, and the doors closed. She pressed the PH button and watched the floor numbers light up as the elevator ascended. When the doors finally opened, Lauren whispered, "*Thank God.*" The palms of her hands were wet.

She stepped out from the elevator and fished her key ring out of her black leather shoulder bag. She found the key Craig had given her and opened the wood paneled door. Walking into the darkened reception area, she listened for the presence of any employees working late. She heard no one, but the office was not in total darkness. She could see that a light was on somewhere beyond the room she was in. Her eyes adjusted to the dimness and she looked around. She was expecting trendy leather couches and love seats, but instead found a beautiful upholstered sofa and side chairs in rich jewel tones. In the center of the room was a brass sculpture of a dolphin with a glass top to serve as a table. On top of it were popular magazines, which were placed there as a courtesy to visitors who were kept waiting. The floors were polished marble which reflected the little light that was spilling in from the hallway. On the walls she noticed art from the Pop Art movement. She recognized Warhol's "Marilyn," a Jasper Johns flag painting, and a Roy Lichtenstein's "Crying Girl." She wondered if they were authentic or reproductions. She wasn't going to take the time to check.

From the reception area, there were two hallways the led from either direction. Lauren walked on her tip toes so her heels wouldn't make a sound on the marble. She chose the hallway to her right, the source of the light. She was grateful that floor here was carpeted to muffle her footsteps. On both sides of the hallway, there were secretary desks in front of each private office. Lauren pulled a small flashlight from her shoulder bag and shone the light into the trash basket. *Good, the cleaning people have already been here, if you can call emptying out the trash cleaning,* Lauren thought.

At the end of the hall, she found the source of light: A large corner office where the lamp on the secretary's desk was left on. From where she stood, she figured the layout of the office space was a U shape. She directed the beam of light into the office and zeroed in on the name plate on the huge executive desk. Theodore R. Bomar, it read. Lauren wondered what the R stood for, maybe Roosevelt. Lauren decided to walk the hallway before going into Bomar's office, just to make sure she was alone. As she shone the light into each office, she found it peculiar that every desktop in the office was neat and orderly. She wondered if there was edict in place.

Lauren returned to Bomar's office, but before entering, she tried to open the pencil drawer of his secretary's desk, hoping to find the file cabinet key. It didn't budge. Lauren tried all the drawers, hoping that one might be left open. Each drawer resisted Lauren's efforts.

Lauren entered Bomar's office and shone the light around the room looking for the filing cabinet. The walls were paneled half way to a chair rail in polished rosewood and elaborate millwork edged the ceiling. The rest of the wall was painted in a deep teal blue. Behind the desk was a built-in wall unit which displayed *object d'art* and hardcover books. Lauren was surprised that she didn't see a metal file cabinet, but thought perhaps the file cabinet was camouflaged behind a door.

On either end of the wall unit were tall cabinet doors. She tried the brass knob on the cabinet door on the left side. It was locked. She tried the cabinet door on the right and it opened easily. Inside, she found a wet bar complete with a sink and small refrigerator/freezer. Glass shelves held cut-crystal bar glasses and there were bottles of liquor lined up like bowling pins. There also was a small wooden wine rack that held about a dozen bottles of wine, all vintage she was sure. With her nerves as frazzled as they were, she wanted a drink, but she didn't dare. She closed the cabinet door and went back to the locked cabinet. She retrieved her key ring which held a ladies version of the Swiss Army knife. She hoped she could pick the lock with either the toothpick or tweezers. She tried the miniature tweezers and after a couple of tries, Lauren unlocked the door. She pulled the door open revealing a four-drawer metal filing cabinet. To Lauren's surprise, the metal cabinet was not locked. Lauren started with the top drawer, having no idea of the organization of Bomar's filing system. She hoped everything was filed alphabetically. She looked under the tab folder for B and found a file folder labeled Broward County School Board. This was her lucky day. Inside was a letter to the associate superintendent for construction, Roy Fernandez, and a proposal. That was easy enough to find the letter, now where do I find the file on the toxic site? Lauren wondered. I didn't think to ask Craig where to look. Maybe if I had an address of the property.

Lauren thumbed through the proposal and found the address of the property. It was in Pompano Beach so Lauren tried the second and then the third drawer looking for it under P. She found the P tab folder but no file folder labeled Pompano Beach. Perhaps it's under pending projects, she surmised. Sure enough, there was a file folder labeled "pending projects--Mediterranean Village." She pulled the file folder halfway out of the drawer and glanced through it. It was the project Bomar was seeking approval from the city commission. She pushed the folder back into its place. She inspected the rest of the drawers, hoping the folder would reveal itself. No such luck, but she did find a file folder labeled personal photo. In it were a dozen or so glossy head shots of Bomar which were used for press releases. She took one and Lauren exited Bomar's office looking for a photocopy machine. She found one a few feet beyond the secretary's desk. She tapped the power button and waited for the light to tell her the machine was ready to copy. After she made copies of the contents of the school board file folder, Lauren turned off the machine and returned the file folder to its place. She closed the drawer and cabinet door. She figured the file folder she was still looking for wasn't in Bomar's office, but was with him in a briefcase.

Walking down the hall, she clutched the copies and photo to her chest. She prayed she wouldn't encounter anyone on her way out. Just a few feet from the receptionist area, Lauren heard a click. She froze in place. The noise was hardly audible and she thought perhaps she was imagining things. She waited, listening, wondering if someone was in the receptionist area. Slowly she walked to the edge of the hallway and peeked around the corner. She didn't see anyone. She quickly walked to the door and let herself out, locking the door behind her. At the elevators, she looked up at the lights above the doors to see if there was any activity. Seeing none, she pushed the call button. The doors opened immediately. She got in and pushed the button for the lobby. The doors closed, but the elevator didn't descend. She pushed the button to open the doors. The doors opened. She pushed the button for the lobby again and the doors closed. Again, the elevator did not descend. Lauren hit the lobby button again. Still nothing happened. Lauren felt her blouse dampen under her arms and she licked her lips. She hit the button to open the doors again and this time she got out. *I don't want to get trapped in this elevator,* she thought. *Maybe I can bring another elevator up to this floor.*

The elevator door closed behind her. Lauren pushed the call button again and the same elevator door opened.

Now what am I going to do? Lauren looked around and saw an exit sign. *I rather take the stairs than be stuck in an elevator anytime,* she thought. *Maybe security locked the elevators downstairs.*

Lauren pushed the door open to the stairs and started walking down, the sound of her footsteps echoing against the grey cinderblock walls. She put one hand on the hand rail to steady herself. She hated walking down the stairs in high heels and she wondered how many flights of stairs there were until she reached the lobby. There was a flight of stairs, a landing, and then another flight of stairs. She figured there were two flights of stairs to every floor. She guessed there were 14 or 15 floors in the building. She continued to plod along, and beads of sweat dampened her bangs. The stairwell was hot and stuffy. Walking down so many stairs and landings had the effect of a winding staircase. The stairs seemed to zoom up at her and she began to feel dizzy and unsure of her footing. She stopped, took off her high heels, and held her pumps by the heels along with the photocopies. She heard footsteps from above and then it was quiet. She immediately panicked. She had no idea who also would be taking the stairs and she didn't want to wait to find out. She assumed someone was following her. With one hand on the railing, Lauren took the stairs as fast as she could without falling. She then heard the footsteps again, only they, too, had picked up speed. Landing after landing, Lauren continued down the stairs. Her heart felt as if it would burst through her chest and she was sweating. She had no idea how far away the footsteps were and she wished she could fly.

Finally, the stairs ended in a short hallway and Lauren ran to the exit door. She pushed the door open and found herself in the back of the building in the parking garage. The garage was empty except for one dark colored van parked a few feet from her. She ran out of the parking garage and onto the empty street which ran parallel to Alhambra. She looked back, but didn't see anyone. She would have to go around the block to get to her car. She continued running down Salzedo Street and then turned the corner to Alhambra. Her car was a welcome sight. She unlocked the car, threw her purse, shoes and papers across the seat and got in. She locked the doors and looked around the street. Except for cars driving by, Lauren saw no one on foot. She was out of breath and her hands trembled. She started the car and backed out of the parking space. She wondered if she should go home, but she was afraid she would be followed. She tried to calm herself and to think rationally about the footfalls in the stairwell. With the elevators malfunctioning, it easily could have been an employee stuck like she was whose only alternative was the stairs. Lauren took a deep breath and exhaled slowly. She drove to the traffic light at Le Jeune Road and was grateful she had the green light. She made a left turn and headed to U.S.1. She glanced in her rearview mirror searching for a dark van. She didn't see one and she hoped she wouldn't. She didn't want to give anyone a chance to tail her so she picked up her speed and passed cars left and right. If she was being followed, she hoped her evasive action would help her.

Now at U.S. 1, she turned right on the red light, not wanting to waste any time. She wondered if someone really had been after her in the stairwell or if she was just being paranoid.

Chapter 18

"Julio. You got good news for me?" Ted Bomar asked. He sat in an aubergine leather chair in the main salon of *Bomar's Bounty*, sipping a vodka martini on the rocks. He had changed out of the business suit he had worn to the office and now sported a black and tan print silk sport shirt, black gabardine slacks, and black Italian leather loafers without socks.

Julio had just arrived at six o'clock and he stood before Ted dressed in a grey tank top and shorts, his beefy arms crossed in front of his massive chest, evidence of daily workouts at Gold's Gym. A black leather fanny pack was secured around his waist and a cell phone was in a case clipped to the waistband of his shorts. "No, man. I haven't seen Craig no wheres. Too bad the story made the news. Otherwise, he wouldn't have a clue, and I could've nailed him. But the guy's smart and he took off. Wouldn't you?"

"I'm the one asking questions here, understand?" Bomar leaned forward in his chair and glared at the five-foot-ten Cuban-American hulk.

Julio's dark eyes stared back at Ted and his mouth curled into a smirk beneath his mustache. "Relax, man. Just making conversation."

Ted sat back and took another swallow of his drink. "I'd just like to know where Craig Richards is. I'm sure he's seen the paper about the poor bastard who got nailed instead of him. And he knows he crossed me on a certain matter. I'm just thinking. What if he contacts the widow? I mean, I wouldn't. I'd just clean out my bank account and get out of Miami. But Craig, I don't know. Something tells me———."

"The widow, huh? Maybe that's who that was."

Ted stood up from his chair. "What the hell are you talking about?"

"Last night, at Craig's house. I've been house sittin', like you said. I see this woman take the mail out of the box last night. Maybe it was her."

Ted charged like a bull toward Julio and in his face yelled, "Why didn't you call me and tell me about it, you idiot? Didn't you think it odd that someone would take someone's mail? Shit. You could have followed her! Damn! She brought the mail to him and you did nothing! Don't you ever think? What do you have between your ears? Shit for brains! Damnit!"

"Sorry, man." Julio stepped back and put his large hands palms up to protect himself. "Relax. You said to camp out at Craig's in case he came back for his shit."

Ted noticed Julio's defensive posture and tried to compose himself. "You're a dumb shit, you know it? I bet Craig contacted the widow and told her everything. Who knows what they're up to? But I'll tell you something. I don't intend to wait and find out. I've already waited long enough. Now I want you to find the bitch and find out where Craig is so you can finish him off. Hell, you're going to have to get rid of her, too. She could go to the police."

"How am I supposed to find her?" Julio asked.

"What kind of dumb shit are you anyway? Do a search on your phone for Michael Casey, you numb skull."

Julio used the app on his mobile phone and found a free directory search. "There's more than one Michael Casey."

"How many?" Ted barked.

"Three."

"Read the addresses."

Julio read them aloud. One was a street in North Miami, another was in Miami and the third was in Kendall, a suburban area southwest of Miami.

"It's got to be the one in Kendall. That's the closest address to the Grove," Ted said. "Call the number and ask to speak to Michael Casey. If it's the right one, a woman will tell you he's deceased."

Julio picked up the portable phone and dialed the number. "I got an answering machine."

"A woman's voice?"

Julio shook his head yes.

"Process of elimination. Hang up and try the other two," Ted said. He finished his drink, threw out the ice in the sink at the wet bar, and made another one. He considered offering a drink to Julio, but changed his mind.

Julio called the other two listings. With the first one, a young girl answered and said she'd get her daddy. Julio hung up before she had the chance. With the second, a man answered and identified himself as Michael Casey. Just to have something to say, Julio asked him which long distance telephone company he was using, and the guy hung up on him.

"I found two Michael Caseys who are alive. That leaves the Kendall address." Julio put down the phone.

"Then go. But be smart on this one. You've got to find out from the wife where Craig is first, remember that?"

"Yeah, sure, man. I'm out of here. I'll find her and I'll get her to talk," Julio said.

"Wait a minute. On second thought, maybe you need some help. Why don't you get one of your buddies from the gym to help you? Is there one you can trust?"

"Yeah, but it's gonna cost you extra. I'll ask Sal."

"What do you mean extra? You screwed up the first time."

"Yeah, I know. But it's not right. You asking me to whack another person in addition to Craig. So that's extra. Plus you can't expect me to pay Sal out of my own pocket."

Ted stared hard at Julio. "All right. How much?"

"Ten each."

"That's twenty thou. You're out of your mind! Fifteen for both of you."

Julio thought about it. "All right."

Ted hesitated and then said. "Wait. I have an idea. I think you should listen in on her phone conversations first. This way, you may get a fix on where Craig is without having to confront her. She may just lead you to him and not even realize it."

"Good idea. Consider it done."

"Okay, then get out of here. And don't screw up."

Julio turned to leave and then stopped. "I'm going to need a deposit."

"What?"

"Come on, man. Don't act surprised. That's the way we do business," Julio pleaded.

"All right." Ted reached in his pants pocket and pulled out a money clip which secured a wad of cash. He peeled off four crisp, thousand dollar bills and handed them to Julio. "Now get out."

Julio left the main salon and at the threshold to the gangplank, he bumped into a tall man in his mid-forties. He had blond hair and his face had a weathered look that came from spending too much time in the sun. His crisp white uniform with epaulets at the shoulders identified him as the captain of *Bomar's Bounty*. "Sorry, Chris. I didn't see you."

"No harm," Chris said, looking around Julio for Ted.

"Then I'm out of here." Julio's bounded down the gangplank.

Entering the salon, Chris asked, "Mr. Bomar. Ready to depart?"

"Not quite. My guest hasn't arrived yet." Ted looked over at Mary who was busy getting the china, silverware and crystal out of the cabinet to set the table for dinner. "Mary, did Richard print out the menu for tonight yet?"

"Yes. Let me get it from the galley." Mary returned in a moment. She read the printed menu. "Appetizer, clams casino. Entree, salmon papillotes with herbs, roasted garlic mashed potatoes, roasted asparagus and a mixed green salad with balsamic vinaigrette. Dessert is chocolate cake. I'll be putting out a variety of hors d'oeuvres before dinner is served, including olive focaccia. "

"Chocolate, a wonderful aphrodisiac," Ted said, laughing. He was thinking of the date Julio arranged for the evening. Julio said she was a thirty-year-old divorcee who he had seen out at the gym since the beginning of the year. He said she was a working girl, but not "that" kind of working girl. He had to hand it to Julio to know how to pick the broads. He hadn't been disappointed in a date yet.

"What time are you expecting your guest to arrive?" Chris asked.

"Oh, I expect her by seven o'clock. I sent the limo for her."

"Very good, sir. I'll be out on the fly bridge," Chris said walking up the spiral staircase.

Ted picked up the cell phone and dialed the code for his home. He had such a hectic day that he had neglected to call his wife earlier. Esther picked up on the first ring. "Hello."

"Esther. It's me. What's going on?"

"Nothing much here, dear. What time will you be home tonight?"

"That's why I'm calling. I've got a feeling this dinner meeting is going to run late so I'm going to be staying on the boat tonight. Will you be all right?"

"Of course, Ted. I always am. I picked up a couple of new DVDs today. I'll watch one of them tonight."

"All right, then. I'll call you tomorrow."

"Okay. I hope everything goes well."

"Thanks, have a good night," Ted said. He hung up and sat there thinking about the evening ahead. He expected it to go very well indeed.

Chapter 19

Julio parked his black Corvette in the lot of Vinnie's Bar & Grill in Coconut Grove. Just about every parking place was taken, confirming that Vinnie's was still popular with the happy hour crowd, mostly young, single professionals in their twenties and thirties. Julio locked the car and walked through the fenced courtyard to the front door. On a Friday night, when the bar was packed with enough people to warrant a fire code citation, patrons crowded this area as well, drinking and flirting, and looking for love. Even for a Tuesday night at 7:15 all bar stools were taken, forcing other people to stand behind those that were seated. Every few minutes a name was announced over the public address system that the party's table was ready for dinner. The dining room was at the rear of the restaurant and it did excellent business as well. The menu offered the standard American fare of fresh-caught Florida fish, prime beef, chicken, some pasta dishes, and salads. Each evening, the chef's specials were handwritten on a black board and displayed on an easel at the hostess's station. Stone crabs were in season and Julio reminded himself to come back one night and order them served with mustard sauce.

Just as he expected, Julio found Sal sitting at the bar. He was putting the moves on a tall blond that reminded him of an actress whose name escaped him. She was striking to say the least.

"Sal, my man, *que pasa?*" Julio asked, tapping Sal on the shoulder.

Sal spun around on his bar stool. Except for the diamond stud in his one ear, he looked like a marine recruit with buzz cut hair. Like Julio, he well-muscled. "Hey, Julio, good to see you. How'd you know I was here?"

"I figured I'd find you here or at Ferguson's."

Sal looked down at Julio's shorts and said, "You just come from Gold's?"

"Nah." Julio nodded his head. "Come outside with me. I need to talk to you."

Sal frowned. "Can't you see I'm busy?"

"Believe me, Sal. This is important. And it's worth your time."

"But my name is on the waiting list for dinner. I'm probably next. I'm dying for those stone crabs. And a piece of key lime pie for dessert."

"Forget the stone crabs and dessert. This is more important," Julio said. Then leaning closer to Sal's ear, he whispering, "Is she your date?"

Sal shook his head no.

Julio gave him an earnest look. "Say goodbye, Sal."

"All right." Sal turned to the blond and said. "I got to go. It was nice to talk to you. You come here often? Maybe I'll see you here again."

The blond smiled sweetly, "Sure, I'll be back Friday night."

Sal got off the bar stool and threw three ten-dollar bills on the bar. He caught the bartender's eye who was serving a long neck beer with a slice of lime to a red-haired lawyer who was a regular at Vinnie's. "Hey, Brian. I got to go. This here is for my drink and give the lady another of whatever she's drinking. Keep the change."

Brian smiled. "Thanks, Sal. See you later."

Sal followed Julio out the door into the pleasant night air. "So what's so damn important that you had to pull me away? Things were going pretty good. And now I don't get to eat stone crabs. And I'm hungry!"

"Oh, shut up. I'll go through a drive-thru and pick us up something to eat."

"So tell me, what's so important that it couldn't wait until after dinner?"

The Deadly Game

"Get in the car. I'll tell you on the way." Julio unlocked his car and released the door lock on the passenger side.

Once the two men were buckled in, Julio started the car and drove out of the parking lot. "I got a job for us. For now, it's a little surveillance job."

"You pulled me away from that honey for this?"

"Yeah, 'cause I'll need you later for more serious stuff."

"Look, Julio. You're putting me in a bad mood. Give it to me straight. What's the job and how much?"

"Remember the job I screwed up? Whacked the wrong guy. Well, I've got to make it right. I've got to find out where the guy's hiding out so I'm goin' to listen in on the widow's phone conversations. Bomar thinks she's helping out Craig and knows where he is. She's sure to talk to him. We listen in; we find out their plans. Then we can take care of the situation. You know what I mean?"

"Yeah, sure. But what if she doesn't talk to him. Then what?"

"Then we'll cross that bridge when we come to it."

"Which is?"

"So maybe we'll have to pressure her to talk. You know how to do that, Sal."

Sal nodded his head. "Yeah, so does Bomar want them both out?"

"You got it."

"For how much?"

"Fifteen thou."

"Each! Great man!"

"No, for the both of us. We split it fifty-fifty."

Sal frowned. "Ah, shit, man. Why did you agree to that? You never stand up to that guy. You gotta get more money."

"Listen, Sal. I rather work for a little less and not have the guy turn on me. You don't know what he's capable of. Especially since Bomar's none too happy with me with the last screw-up. I don't think this will take a lot of time. We're dealing with a suburban housewife here."

"All right. I don't like it, but I can use the money."

"Good."

"So did you get some money up front?" Sal asked.

"What do you take me for? An idiot? Of course." Julio drove with one hand on the wheel and with the other, unzipped the fanny pack and fished out two thousand dollar bills. "Here's yours."

"Two thousand. That's it?"

"Look, Ted's pissed. I don't need to provoke him. We'll get the rest when the job is done. Trust me."

"Fine. So how are you going to listen to her phone conversations? You going to break in to tap her phone? That's illegal, you know." Sal smiled.

"Aren't you the comedian? Don't have to man." Julio laughed. "I have a radio scanner."

"What if she sees us?"

"We don't have to be right outside her door. This thing will pick up her conversation a block away."

"No kidding? I just may get one of those for myself. Could be fun. You never know what kind of conversations you might hear," Sal laughed.

"Hey, you're my friend. You can borrow this one when we're done."

"Thanks, Julio.

In a matter of minutes, Julio drove in the parking lot of Dadeland Mall and parked the Vet at the southeast entrance.

"Sal, there's the hamburger joint in the mall," Julio said. He released the seat belt buckle and took a twenty dollar bill from his fanny pack and handed it to Sal. "Why don't you go in and get whatever you want to eat."

"Okay. What do you want?" Sal asked, releasing his seat belt.

"Ah, I don't know. I shouldn't eat a hamburger. Too much fat. Get me two grilled chicken breast sandwiches and a large iced tea."

"Want fries?"

"Naw. Gotta cut down."

"All right, then. See you back here in a few minutes."

Julio sat fantasizing how easy the job was going to be. He was figuring the widow and Craig would set up a rendezvous and he would follow them. Hopefully, he could finish them off at the same time. If not, maybe he and Sal would split up, each going after one of them. Waiting for Sal, he took the scanner out of the glove box and put new batteries into it. The piece of equipment was black and no bigger than a cell phone. In fact, at a glance, that's exactly what it looked like. The scanner locks into the frequencies of the cordless phones in use in the immediate area, one at a time. There were only a total of ten to go through so it wouldn't take much time. All Julio would have to do is listen and recognize the voice. Of course, he had never heard her voice before, but he figured he would know who she was from the kind of conversations a woman in her situation would have. Once he found her phone frequency, he would just note the number displayed on the screen. He'd be sure to write it down or memorize it. The next time he wanted to eavesdrop on her conversation, he simply would enter the few digits. It would take only a second.

Julio heard a light tapping on the passenger side window. Sal was back with a bag of food, munching on a French fry. Julio released the car lock and Sal got in. Suddenly the car smelled of greasy French fries and hamburgers.

Sal said, "It didn't take you long."

"Naw, they weren't that busy."

Sal put the paper cups of tea in the car's beverage holders and stuck straws into the lids of each. He then pulled out a cheeseburger, unwrapped it, and took a bite. Chewing his food, he said, "You want your sandwich now while you drive?"

"Sure," Julio said. When he drove out of the parking lot, he took the sandwich from Sal, and ate with one hand holding the sandwich, and the other steering the car. By the time he finished eating the sandwich, Julio was turning down Lauren's street. He took a long swallow of his tea, belched, and slowed the car to a crawl. "Look for 8101. It should be on the right side."

"There it is, two more houses down," Sal said, finishing the last of his French fries and drink. "The lights are on. I guess she's home."

"Great. I'm going to park at the end of the block on the other side of the street so we can watch the house," Julio said. He drove to the end of the street, made a U-turn and parked the car along the swale. He shut off the headlights, opened the windows, and shut off the engine. He reached for the scanner and turned it on. He entered 46 on the key pad and then pushed the scan button. "Okay. baby, do your magic. Find her for me."

Chapter 20

From the boat deck, Ted let out a sigh as he watched his driver park the black limousine. It was 7:20 and he was on his third martini. He wondered whether his date was delayed because of work or because she simply couldn't decide what to wear. His driver, Jim, opened the door for the woman and extended his hand to help her out. Watching her emerge from the car, Ted liked what he saw. She was on the tall side, probably five-seven or five-eight, making her taller than Ted, but that didn't bother him. The way he looked at it, all women were the same height once you got them in bed.

The bay breeze picked up the hem of her dress. As she walked, she smoothed her short hair and then checked her earlobes for her earrings. She carried a small evening purse that matched her dress, a clingy number that defined her ample breasts and skimmed over her hips. At first he thought the dress was black, but as she got closer to the gangplank and into the light, it could see it was midnight blue—a stunning choice against her fair skin and red hair. She had a pretty face and something about the way she carried herself told him she was no pushover. Chris met her at the gangplank and took her to meet Ted on the aft deck.

"Ted, this is Judy Miller," Chris said. "Judy, this is Ted Bomar."

Judy cleared her throat. "Did you say Bomar?"

Ted rose from his chair and Judy extended her hand. Instead of shaking it, he kissed the top of it. "That's right. It's a pleasure to meet you. Julio told me you were gorgeous. And he was right."

Judy inhaled deeply and half-smiled. Her brown eyes looked inquisitive, as though she were remembering something. "Err—why, thank you, Ted. When Julio said I'd be meeting you on the boat, I had no idea he was referring to a yacht. This is really impressive."

"I'm glad you like it. Since the weather is so calm tonight, I thought we'd take it out for a cruise and have dinner on board. Would you like the fifty-cent tour before I get you a drink?" Ted held up his glass. "I'm about ready for another one."

"I'd love to." Judy hesitated and then said. "I'm afraid Julio didn't tell me much about you."

Ted slid the door open to the air-conditioned main salon. He allowed Judy to enter the room first and closed the door after him. He watched her face for her reaction. It revealed what he expected. This was a new experience for her.

"This is beautiful, but brrr, it's freezing in here," Judy said, shivering.

"You're right." Ted walked over to the thermostat and adjusted the temperature. "There. That should make it more comfortable."

"Thank you. I don't know if it's a guy thing or what, but it always seems men like the air conditioning colder than women."

Laughing, Ted said, "I guess it's all that hot blood coursing through our veins."

Judy managed a small smile. "I suppose."

"Well, anyhow, as you can see, this is the main salon, dining area, and bar. Over here is the powder room and back around here is the galley," said Ted as he led the way. A chef was busy tearing up Romaine lettuce for a salad. He glanced up from his work and smiled.

"A real professional kitchen," Judy said. She noted the stainless steel cabinets and work surfaces. "This is wonderful."

"Come on," Ted said, reaching for her hand. "I'll show you the staterooms. First the main one. I think you'll like it."

"Staterooms? How many are there?"

"Four, actually. I find it perfect for corporate entertaining."

Judy let him take her hand and followed him on his tour. He showed her his stateroom first and she commented on the beautiful watercolor paintings and the bronze sculpture of a dolphin that was placed on the built-in teak cabinets. Everything was beautifully color coordinated, from the snow white carpeting to the luxurious bedspread in slate gray and ivory. When they returned to the main salon, they found a silver platter of hors d'oeuvres along with linen cocktail napkins on the glass topped cocktail table, the base of which was a giant conch shell in bronze edged in brass. Mary, the stewardess, was standing at the bar.

"Ah, good, I see the hors d'oeuvres are out. Would you care for a drink now, Judy?" Ted said, releasing her hand.

"Sure, I'd like a Seagram's and soda if you have it. Thank you," Judy said, sitting down on the couch. She didn't lean back but perched herself on the edge with her back ramrod straight.

Ted looked to the stewardess to make sure she heard the drink order. "Mary, I'll have another, please." He took a seat on the leather couch a respectable distance from Judy.

Mary served the drinks from a tray and took Ted's empty glass back to the bar.

Ted raised his glass toward her in a toast. "Here's to new beginnings."

They clinked their glasses and Ted took a long swallow. Judy sipped her drink and eyed Ted as he picked up a small gift-wrapped package from the end table. Judy's eyes widened in surprise.

Handing the package to her, Ted said, "I hope you like it."

"How sweet of you." Judy carefully removed the small red bow and silver foil paper. "Oh, my. Joy perfume." She opened the box and pulled out the crystal flacon of the perfume. Unsealing the bottle, she dabbed the perfume at her pulse points. "Mm. This is lovely. Thank you so much. That was a very thoughtful thing to do."

Ted gave Judy a broad smile. "I'm glad you're pleased. It's a classic fragrance, like Chanel No. 5."

Ted took the olive from his martini and popped it into his mouth. "I love olives. If you like olives, have the focaccia."

"It looks delicious," Judy said, reaching for the hors d'oeuvre on the coffee table before her. She took a bite. "Delicious."

Ted helped himself as well and then inched closer on the couch next to Judy.

"So what do you do, Judy? Are you a model?" Ted asked.

"Oh, no. Not me. I'm not thin enough," Judy said. She sipped her cocktail.

"A flight attendant, then?"

"I don't think so."

"An actress?"

"Stop already."

"Well, you're very pretty. Do you work?"

"Yes, I'm an art director."

"Who do you work for?"

She paused and said, "Ah, I'm a free-lancer, actually. I have a studio in my house. I like it that way. I can make my own hours."

Ted studied her. He sensed her nervousness. "I see. Have you ever worked on any real estate accounts?"

"Ah....no."

The sound of the yacht's engine interrupted Ted's thoughts. "It sounds like we're getting under way. Why don't we go back out on deck?"

Judy followed Ted out of the main salon. Mary followed them out, carrying the silver platter of food and placing it on the table which had been set for dinner. She returned to the main salon leaving Judy and Ted alone. The air temperature was a pleasant 75 degrees, perfect weather for an evening on the water.

Judy said, "The table looks beautiful."

"Mary did a wonderful job as usual," Ted said, gesturing to the setting. Fine Lenox china, Orefors crystal wine glasses and silver flatware on a white linen tablecloth were illuminated by four cut-crystal votives. A crystal vase held freshly cut pink tulips. They each took a seat. Chris had already maneuvered the yacht from its slip and they were underway. The breeze fluttered the edges of the table cloth.

"Have another focaccia," Ted said as he reached for one himself.

"I think I'll try a stuffed mushroom. They look delicious." Judy helped herself. "So Ted, Julio didn't tell me much about you except that you owned your own business, and that you knew how to treat a lady. In fact, he didn't even tell me your last name. What kind of business do you own?"

"I'm a real estate developer. Ever hear of Mirabella?"

Judy nodded her head. "Ah, so that's why you wanted to know if I've worked on a real estate account."

Ted smiled. "I thought I could give you a project to work on, maybe do a logo design for my Mediterranean village."

"You must have an ad agency. Isn't that something they would do for you?"

"Yes, but it's always good to see what other ideas are out there."

"But don't you have a contract with the agency?"

"Yes. But what's the difference? If I want to see what you come up with and I pay you, what the big deal?"

"I don't know. I would just think it might upset the people you work with at the agency."

"Don't worry about it." Ted drained the vodka martini, the ice cubes tinkling in the glass. "Are you ready for another drink?"

"I guess," Judy said, taking another swallow of her highball.

Ted held up his glass and shook it, the ice cubes signaling he was ready for refills. Instantly, the stewardess appeared and refreshed their drinks from the wet bar where they were seated on the aft deck. "Here you are, Mr. Bomar."

"Thank you, Mary."

"What time would you like me to serve dinner?"

"After this drink, if you will."

"Certainly, sir," Mary said, exiting to the main salon. She closed the glass door behind her. Light jazz played through the outdoor speakers.

"So tell me about Mirabella, Ted. I'm just familiar with the one community in Kendall."

"What's to tell? I've built homes all over the state of Florida. I've been doing it for thirty years. I sold out every community I started. I also own commercial property. But I really don't feel like talking business tonight. Look at the skyline," Ted said, raising his glass in the direction of the coastline. "Beautiful, isn't it? No wonder they call Miami 'The Magic City.' It does look magical with all the lights."

"Yes, beautiful, but who can afford to live here? It takes almost two paychecks to pay for monthly housing, something like forty-three percent. And instead of building more affordable housing, all you see are luxury high-rises going up. It's a disgrace."

"Foreign nationals buy the expensive properties. If they didn't there wouldn't be a market for them," Ted said, wondering what he could say to get Judy's mind off such serious matters. The other women he'd gone out with in the past were more willing playmates. They would flirt and by now they would be making body contact with him, whether it would be brushing a breast against him or putting a hand on his thigh. This one was really reserved and was certainly not going to make the first move. He wondered what he could do to make her loosen up. "Judy, tell me. Do you like to travel?"

Sipping her drink, she said, "Sure, I do. But that takes money."

"Tell me where you'd like to go."

"I'd love to go to Europe. Paris, maybe. Florence. Venice."

"Ah, yes, as an artist, those cities would intrigue you. Have you considered something a little closer? Like the Bahamas or the Caribbean?" Ted said, taking her hand in his. He saw her body stiffen and with his other hand, turned her face toward him. He looked into her eyes and thought he saw

146

fear. She removed his hand from her face and looked away. With her free hand, she reached for her glass and took a long swallow.

"Sure."

"Would you like to go, maybe some weekend?"

Judy swallowed, "I don't know. Maybe after I get to know you better."

"Well, I hope we'll get to know each other a lot better tonight," Ted said, giving her his most charming smile. "Forgive me for saying so, but you seem very nervous. Do I make you nervous, Judy?"

"Oh no, I'm sorry to give you that impression. I got divorced not too long ago and I don't date very much. It's just *the idea* of dating makes me nervous," Judy said, laughing.

"All right, then." Ted heard the door to the salon open and he released Judy's hand. Mary stepped out on deck with a tray holding their salads, a basket of rolls, and molded butters with the initials TRB.

"I hope you're ready, Mr. Bomar," Mary said.

Draining his martini, Ted said, "Perfect timing, Mary. You have it down to a science."

"Thank you, sir," Mary said. She put the salads at each place and placed the rolls and butter within Ted's reach. "Shall I serve the wine now, Mr. Bomar?"

"Certainly." Turning to Judy, he said, "They say wine doesn't go with salad because of the vinegar. I don't pay any attention to that."

Mary left as silently as she had arrived and within moments she was back with an ice bucket holding a bottle of *Pouilly Fuisee.* She opened the wine earlier so she simply poured some wine in Ted's goblet and waited for his approval before pouring wine into Judy's glass.

After tasting the wine, he said, "Very nice. I think you'll enjoy it, but there's no hurry. Finish your drink first, if you like."

He offered Judy some bread and she accepted. He passed her the monogrammed butter rounds.

"Those are your initials on the butter. Nice," Judy said, helping herself to a pat of butter. "I see that the china and silverware also have your monogram. Who made your china for you?"

"Lenox, of course."

"What do you mean, of course?"

"I insist on doing business with an *American* company."

"Oh, I see," Judy said, thinking for a moment. "Do you drive a Mercedes or a Cadillac?"

"What are you getting at?" Ted asked, feeling provoked. If he didn't know better, if would believe she was trying to start an argument.

"Oh, never mind. I'm just being silly. You know, some people insist on only buying American-made things, yet they drive a foreign-built car. I think it's hypocritical."

"I suppose you're right. I don't even know why I made of point of saying it was an American company. The silver and crystal aren't American." Ted said, trying to ease himself out of a disagreement. He knew an argument would end the evening early. He stabbed at his salad and put a fork full of greens into his mouth. "Wonderful. There's nothing like a good Balsamic vinegar. Do you like arugula?"

Tasting the salad, Judy said, "Yes, I do. The arugula, romaine and the variety of other greens makes the salad more interesting."

Throughout the rest of the meal, Ted avoided topics he thought might ignite controversy. They talked about movies, music, and their favorite plays. He found out she loved any movie with Leonard Di Caprio or Denzel Washington in it, hated rap music, and didn't go to the theater much because she thought the price of admission was too high. He didn't offer to take her since he couldn't risk being seen with her. After all, Esther's friends attended the theater regularly, whether it was the Adrienne Arsht Center, the Jackie Gleason Theater for the Performing Arts or the Broward Center for the Performing Arts.

They had just finished dessert when they heard the muffled sound of a telephone ringing. A moment later, Mary appeared with the cell phone. "Mr. Bomar. You have a phone call. It's Julio. Do you want to take it?"

"Yes, yes, I do," Ted said, grabbing the phone from the stewardess' hand. She poured more coffee into their cups from a silver coffeepot and then silently cleared the dessert dishes.

"Julio. What's the word?" Ted asked. "Lauren, huh? There are lots of condos in Naples. Did you get an idea which one?" Ted paused. "Hands off for now. Have Sal keep an eye out. And you. Finish the job in Naples. Call me when you're done."

Ted broke the connection and laid the phone down on the table. He felt Judy staring at him and wondered how much she picked up on his conversation.

"Excuse me, but I couldn't help but hear. What was that all about?" Judy asked, her face showing concern.

"Oh, nothing. Absolutely nothing," Ted said, smiling. He cupped her chin in his hand. "Would you like an after-dinner drink? Some Amaretto, perhaps?"

Chapter 21

"All right, Sal," Julio said, ending his call with Ted. "I'll take you back to your car and then I'm going to Naples. You heard her, man. She says to him, 'How do you like the Gulf Shore Vista?'" Julio laughed. "This should be a piece of cake. Anyways, I'm goin' to finish off Craig and you get your car and keep an eye out for her. I doubt she'll go anywhere tonight. But keep your distance. I don't want her calling the cops. Call me on my cell if you need me."

Julio checked the glove box for his .38 Special before starting the car and driving back to Coconut Grove. On the way, all Julio heard from Sal was how he wasn't getting to eat his stone crabs and why should he have to sit in his car all night watching some stupid bitch's house.

When Julio pulled into the parking lot of Vinnie's Bar and Grill, the parking lot was still full. Sal got out of the car and rather than walk to his car, he headed to the restaurant. Julio put down the window and yelled, "Where the hell do you think you're going?"

Sal spun on his heels and glared at Julio. "The men's room. What's it to you?"

"Well, don't get any ideas about staying here. I want you back at the house. You hear me?"

Sal flipped Julio his middle finger and turned. He marched into the restaurant without turning back.

You just better go back to her house or you're goin' to have to deal with me! Julio thought as he revved the engine, put the car in gear, and drove out of the parking lot, tires squealing. He drove to Kendall Drive to get on the Florida Turnpike. From there he could access I-75 which would take him right into

Naples. But first he would stop at a gas station and fill up. He remembered that it was at least a two-hour drive to Naples and he didn't know if there were any gas stations along I-75.

The drive to Naples was relatively quick and easy. He remembered the days when the only way to get to Naples from Miami was U.S. 41. Stop and go with the traffic lights. I-75 was a superhighway with super speeds. It seemed no one observed the seventy-miles-per-hour speed limit. He had to consciously watch his speed. Periodically, the Florida Highway Patrol cracked down on speeders. Fines were hefty and there were always points that were put on one's driving record.

He found the Gulf Shore Vista condominium without much trouble. Once he got off I-75 and made his way onto U.S. 41, he entered it into his maps app on his cell phone. It was located on Gulf Shore Boulevard. He was at the condo in a matter of ten minutes. It was just a four-story stucco building in a U-shape with the closed part of the U facing the street. He figured inside the U was a communal swimming pool. There was parking on both sides of the building. He drove in and looked for a place to park. Every space had an assigned number. At the end of the parking lot, he had a view of the water. There was a small bay with docks leading from the bulkhead. He pulled into an assigned parking space, then thought better of it and backed out. He tried the other side of the parking lot and found one precious guest space available. He parked, cut his headlights, and let the engine idle for a few minutes trying to decide what to do. He didn't know what apartment number Craig was in and he couldn't just go knocking on doors.

Damn, the parking place, Julio thought. *If I knew what kind of car Craig is driving, maybe I could find out the apartment number. I don't dare call Ted at this time. He's probably in bed right about now. And I don't need any more of his shit! Asshole! Cabrón.*

Julio turned off the ignition and got a small card and pen out of his fanny pack. He got out and walked along the parking lot, noting the numbers of the parking spaces that the cars occupied. Having done that, he went into the breezeway where he guessed he would find a bank of mail boxes. He was right. From his notes, it appeared there was only one parking space per unit, the parking place number was the same number as the apartment. With all the snowbirds down for the winter, he realized this was not going to be easy without knowing what kind of car Craig was driving. He figured he had a choice to wait and hope to see Craig entering or leaving the building or call Ted in the morning. Either way, he had to wait. At this hour, things were pretty quiet.

He walked into the courtyard. There was an Olympic-size illuminated swimming pool that took center stage. Tables with umbrellas and chairs along with lounges were spread out on the deck. The perimeter was professionally landscaped with bird of paradise, heliconia, bromeliads and bougainvillea. Spotlights focused on Queen Anne palms added to the ambience. Julio noted the place was immaculate indicating a resident manager. He looked at the ground level units and saw one nearest to the bayside with Manager on the door. He wondered if someone was watching him. Julio knew that just the fact that he was young made him conspicuous. Naples was known as a rich retirement haven. He decided to go back to his car and wait.

He had been sitting in his car for about two hours when a tall silver-haired senior dressed in a yellow polo shirt and yellow plaid golf shorts approached his car. He was carrying a flashlight and shined the light on Julio's license tag. He walked to Julio's open window and asked, "Are you waiting for someone?"

Taken by surprise, Julio stammered, "err, yes...I...uh."

"Who are you waiting for?" the silver-haired senior demanded.

"Who wants to know?"

"I'm the manager and I want to know."

"I, uh, waiting for my Aunt Rosalie," Julio said.

"Rosalie who?"

Julio thought he might be able to pull off a lie. "Rosalie Kaplan."

The Deadly Game

"Rosalie Kaplan. There's no one here by that name."

"Ah, I was thinking Kaplan, but she remarried recently. I don't remember her new husband's name."

"Look, my friend. There's no Rosalie that lives here. You probably have the wrong address. So I'm going to have to ask you to leave. You're taking up one of the few guest spots available."

"No problem. I'll try calling her." Julio turned on the ignition and the Corvette roared to life. Condo police, he thought as he backed out of the parking space and drove on to the street. In his rear view mirror, he saw the senior watching him. He turned right and drove slowly to Park Shore Drive, and then he made a U turn and drove back toward Gulf Shore Vista. Right across the street from the condo was a small parking lot that posted a Beach Parking sign. He backed into a space so he could get an unobstructed view of the condo. He sat there for a long time, just staring, thinking and becoming more agitated by the minute. Naples wasn't his home turf and he didn't like being here. And then there was Ted. He hated working for the cocky, arrogant, and belligerent s.o.b. If anyone else had talked to him the way Ted did, Julio would have broken the guy's nose, or worse. But Julio knew that if he wanted the money, he'd have to put up with Ted's tantrums. He slouched down in the leather seat and put his head back. He wondered if Craig would get up early and go jogging on the beach. That would be a great time to nail him. He yawned and crossed his arms over his chest. His eyelids felt heavy and he thought he just close them for a second.

***

He was awakened by children laughing and birds chirping. The sun was already high in the sky. An elderly couple were walking by with what Julio assumed were their two grandchildren. The little boy and girl were each carrying a yellow float while the grandmother was carrying an insulated bag, undoubtedly filled with snacks and beverages. The man was wearing a fishing cap and sunglasses with a white plastic nose protector. Julio thought those things looked really stupid, almost as stupid as those clip-on sunglasses that flip up from regular glasses. He watched the man struggle with two folded aluminum lounge chairs and a beach umbrella. Julio thought it was amazing the trouble people took to spend a few hours soaking up the sun. When Julio went to Crandon Park on Key Biscayne, all he took was a sand chair and a towel. Anything else he needed he could buy or bum from someone.

Julio cursed himself for falling asleep. The fact that Craig may have left the building by now put him in a foul mood. His neck was stiff, his mouth was dry and he needed a toilet. He wiped the sleep from his eyes and as his hands brushed across his cheeks, he felt the stubble of a beard. He glanced at his watch. It was already nine o'clock Wednesday morning. *These old farts don't waste any time getting to the beach!* Julio thought.

Looking at the condo, he noticed empty parking spaces. For now the business of Craig would have to wait. Julio knew he would still have the advantage of surprise. He started the car and drove over to a fast food place on U.S. 41 for breakfast and to use the men's room. In his haste to get to Naples, he hadn't even packed a toothbrush or a razor. He stared at himself in the men's room mirror. He didn't like looking like a bum, but he had a job to do. He washed his face and hands in the sink and dried them with rough paper towels. A shower and shave also would have to wait. He ordered orange juice, a large coffee, and pancakes with syrup. After breakfast, he returned to the beach parking lot and parked under a palm tree. He checked his watch. It was nine-forty-five He punched in Ted's office number on his cell phone and was connected to him immediately.

"Did you complete your job in Naples?" Ted asked quietly.

"Not yet. What kind of car is he driving?"

"A Toyota Camry. Why?"

Ignoring his question, Julio said with sarcasm, "That narrows it down a lot. What color?"

"Silver, I think. What's the problem, Julio? I thought you would have finished the job by now."

"Look, I don't know what condo unit the guy is in, but if I knew what kind of car, I'd match the parking place number to the apartment number."

"Why didn't you just check the license plates?" Ted asked. "How many cars do you think would have Miami-Dade County tags in Naples?"

"What? You think I didn't look?" Julio said. He took the defense. "Do you know how many dealers put a frame around the tag with their name on it? It covers up the county name. So, yeah, I looked. But I don't go around with a screw driver taking off the frames so I can check out the county."

"Oh, shut up already. Wouldn't most of the plates be out of state anyway you moron? I bet most of the people at the condo are snowbirds. Probably very few Florida plates. Damn it! I'm not going to waste my time arguing with you. I've got work to do. And so do you. Call me when you're finished. No excuses!"

The phone line went dead. Julio clutched the phone, seething with anger. Restraining himself from pitching the cell phone out the window, Julio turned the phone off, and put it in his fanny pack.

He's a real prick talking to me like that. Talking down to me like I'm a two-year-old. After this job, he can get someone else to do his dirty work! Screw him!

He jerked open the glove box, got out his .38 Special, and hid it in the waistband of his shorts under the T-shirt. He knew he was going to have to be careful walking around this condo since the manager got a good look at him last night. Of course, there was the possibility that any one of the residents would call the cops based on Julio's unkempt appearance. Julio locked his car and walked across the street with determination. He found the silver Toyota Camry parked at the end of the lot near the bay. He made a mental note of the parking space number: 216. He didn't want to take the chance of being seen in the courtyard so he took the few steps down to the bulkhead. There was a concrete walkway and two dilapidated wooden docks badly in need of repair. Considering how well maintained the condo was, the docks didn't fit the picture. He wondered if they were scheduled for replacement.

It was already a scorcher of a morning, and the sweat dotted his forehead and trickled down his back. From the waterfront he looked over the hedges into the courtyard hoping he might see Craig lying on a lounge chair. There was only a woman in her mid-sixties pushing her bleached blonde hair into a bathing cap. She wore a black one-piece bathing suit which showed off her deep bronze tan. She was in good shape for her age, Julio thought. He watched her slip into the pool and swim the length.

Julio turned when he heard the engine of an outboard motor. A sportfisher boat cruised by with two couples aboard. They waved at him and he made like he didn't notice, stooping down to retie his athletic shoe. *There must be a pass just south of here*, Julio thought, *for access to the Gulf.* He looked at the two docks in front of him. There was a fourteen-foot sportfisher tied up to the dock on his left. The one directly in front of him was empty. He could see the mooring lines were there so a boat must be out. He wondered about Craig and decided to take a chance by going up to apartment 216 to see if he was there. Rather than walk through the pool area and be noticed, Julio went around the building to the parking lot. At the porte cochère, he walked through the breezeway and then took the stairs to the second floor. The fourth door was 216. He looked around to see if he was being observed and not seeing anyone, he peered into the window. What he saw was the kitchen. There were no lights on in the place, but he could see there was coffee in the glass pot and a box of cereal on the counter. He put his ear to the window and listened. Not a sound. It appeared that Craig had been there, but left. *Where did he go?* He wondered. *Fishing?*

Chapter 22

Lauren was refilling her coffee cup when the phone rang. "Hello."

It was Judy. She sounded nervous. "Oh, thank goodness I finally reached you. I was beginning to worry. I called you last night when I got home and didn't get an answer."

"I was here. What time did you call?"

"It was about one."

"I know I was asleep. I don't think I turned the ringer back on my telephone in the bedroom since last week. I just didn't hear the phone ring."

"I called you again about ten minutes ago."

"I was in the shower. Anyway, you got me now. So what's up? You sound upset. How was your date last night?"

"That's why I'm calling. Oh, Judy. I'm worried about you and Craig."

"Well, I hope so."

"No, Lauren, it's something else! My blind date last night was Ted Bomar."

"What!" Lauren shrieked. "How the hell did that happen?"

"You know I've been going to the gym. There's this guy that hangs out. He offered to fix me up with this guy who owns his own company and has a boat. That sounded good. You know how I love to go out boating. So I said yes."

"You didn't get a name first?"

"Well, yeah, Ted."

"And no last name."

"No."

"Why not?"

157

"He said he couldn't remember."

"And that was good enough for you? I can't wait to hear the rest. Tell me what happened."

"Well, his driver picked me up in a limo and took me to the yacht."

"Yacht? I thought you said boat."

"Yeah, I did, but the boat is a yacht."

"Go on."

"Anyway, I get introduced and find out his name is Ted Bomar. I freaked. I was so nervous. Here I know who he is and what he's done. I was scared to death. I didn't know what to do. I'm on this yacht with him and I could tell he was expecting to—you know. And then I kept thinking about you and your crazy plan, and I was afraid he could read my mind and then—."

"Judy, slow down."

Judy rushed on. "This is the really terrible part. We just finished dinner, and Ted gets a phone call from Julio."

"Who's Julio?"

"The guy at the gym who fixed me up. Anyway, he takes the call right in front of me. Oh, Lauren," Judy groaned.

"What? Tell me already."

"Well, Ted says your name, 'Lauren,' and then says 'there are lots of condos in Naples.' Then he said 'did you get an idea which one?' Then he says 'hands off now. Have Sal keep an eye out.' And then he told Julio to finish the job in Naples and call him when he's done. Somehow he knows where Craig is. Lauren, how would he know?"

After a long pause, Lauren said, "The only way he could know was to have listened to my telephone conversation with Craig last night. God, am I stupid! I even mentioned the name of the condo -- Gulf Shore Vista. How could he have listened? Could my phone be tapped?"

"Lauren, I don't know much about tapping phones but wouldn't someone have to get into your house to do it? And you have an alarm system which would go off if someone tried to break in." Judy paused. "Wait! I just thought of something. You have a cordless phone, don't you?"

"Yes, in my home office. It's part of my answering machine. I always go in there after work to check for messages and then call out on that phone to return calls."

"Are you on that phone now?"

"No, I'm in the kitchen."

"You know how a cordless phone works, don't you?" said Judy not waiting for her to answer. "It works on radio waves. That means someone could pick up your conversation. I know I've picked up on my neighbor's when I'm on my cordless."

"Oh, my dear God. So now you're saying that Julio knows exactly where Craig is, and Ted told him to finish the job on him. Because of my stupid big mouth, he's a sitting duck. Why wasn't I more careful? Why didn't I think?"

"Stop blaming yourself, Lauren. Remember, your life is in danger right now."

"What?"

"He told Sal to keep an eye out. My guess he means an eye out for you. I think that when Craig is out of the way, you're next. Julio knows you're helping Craig so you know too much."

"How'd I get myself into this?" Lauren sank into the kitchen chair. "I'm going to have to get in touch with Craig to warn him, if it isn't already too late."

"All right. I'll let you go. I will see you at work, won't I? I think you're going to be safer there. Check outside for any unusual cars before you leave. And Lauren, maybe you should call the police."

I'll check for cars. I don't know about the police just yet. Let me off the phone so I can call Craig. I'll see you at work."

"Okay, be careful."

After hanging up the phone, Lauren opened the front door to get her daily newspaper and looked up and down the street. If Sal was watching out for her, she wondered where. She didn't see any suspicious cars.

She went back into the house, discarded the plastic bag containing the newspaper in the kitchen trash can, and laid the newspaper on the kitchen table. She picked up the kitchen phone and called the number at the Naples condo. With no answering machine there to pick up her call, the phone rang unanswered. She hung up and this time dialed Craig's cell phone and left a message for him to call her. She wondered if he took her up on her suggestion to go fishing. She had thought about it at bedtime just before turning out the light. She remembered Craig had told her he enjoyed boating so she had called him from her bedroom telephone, not using the cordless, thank goodness. He said he just might do that rather than sit in the apartment all day. He said he'd go out early in the morning when the fish would most likely be biting. She had told him the apartment key would open the storage closet in the condo's breezeway. There he would find everything he needed: life vests, fishing gear, and the key to the boat's ignition.

Lauren sat down at the table and sipped her coffee. Fear enveloped her like a python squeezes its prey. Her life was in danger and so was Craig's. She had to warn him. She hoped he took his cell phone out on the boat and would return the call. But what if he went back to the condo and Julio was waiting for him? Then what? If he kills Craig, I'm next. The whole situation seemed to be beyond her control, but her intuition told her to keep to the game plan. She was too nervous to eat breakfast so she went back to her bathroom to finish getting ready for work.

On the drive into Miami, she glanced in her rearview mirror every few seconds to see if she was being followed. Sal was to keep an eye out for her but where was he? What did he look like? When she turned off the ignition after parking her car, her hands trembled. She wondered if Judy had any tranquilizers with her. Lauren took in a deep breath and exhaled slowly. She repeated the breathing exercise a few more times until she felt herself relax.

When she got to her office, she put her purse in her desk drawer and laid her locked briefcase on the desk. She sat down with a sigh and dialed Craig's cell phone, this time leaving her office telephone number. She wondered how long it would be before she would hear from him. Or if she would at all. She sat down, turned on her computer and checked her email.

There were no messages which was not unusual for the hour of the morning. It was only nine o'clock. She stared at her briefcase and thought about its contents. Craig had congratulated her on her tenacity in securing the folder from Bomar's office and consoled her when she explained that she hadn't found the file on the toxic site. He had assured her that the folder wasn't really all that important since public records would point to Ted Bomar as the owner of the property and soil tests at the site would prove her allegations.

Her thoughts were interrupted by Liz who knocked on the door frame.

Lauren looked up and smiled. "Come in, Liz. What's the matter? Is something wrong?"

Liz's brows were furrowed and her eyes were glistening as though tears would flow any moment. "Gee, Lauren. I really screwed up this time. I can't believe I did such a stupid thing. I'm really sorry. Oh, dear. I'm so sorry."

"Liz, it's all right. Tell me what happened," Lauren said leaning forward in her chair.

"You're going to kill me. Oh, no, I didn't mean that. I mean you're going to hate me."

Lauren frowned. "I won't hate you. Just tell me."

"Well, I just hope you can get it finished in time for the Thursday three o'clock city commissioner's meeting."

Lauren's eyes widened. "Get what finished? You're not talking about the video presentation for Mirabella, are you?"

Liz shook her head slowly. "I'm sorry. I really am."

"Liz, you told me the city commissioner's meeting is Friday at three; not Thursday at three. Today is Wednesday. You're telling me I have one less day?"

Liz shook her head slowly once more. Lauren thought if Liz had been a dog she would have rolled over on her back with her paws up in surrender. "Oh, no, Liz. I don't need this kind of stress. Do you understand? As it is my nerves are shot. Now this?"

Liz just looked at Lauren silently. Lauren hoped Liz wouldn't cry. "How did you make this mistake with the days? Huh? I know it's not going to change anything, but I'm just curious."

In a whisper, Liz said, "This is going to sound stupid, but when I read the memo that it was due on the thirteenth, when I glanced at my monthly desk calendar, I didn't realize I was looking at the wrong month. You see, I was planning when I could go on vacation and I was looking at the month of June. I didn't flip the calendar back to February. The thirteenth falls on a Thursday in February but in June the thirteenth falls on a Friday. So that's why I told you the presentation was Friday."

Lauren shook her head. "That's some explanation. Well, let me think a minute." Lauren rubbed her chin. "I'm supposed to get client approval this morning and do the voice recording this afternoon. Tomorrow morning I'm supposed put the video together and then lay in the audio track. It's possible to complete the video, but there is no time for the client to see the finished product before the meeting. So, I'm going to let *you* explain that to Bill Parsons. Obviously, the client is operating on the belief that the meeting is and always has been Thursday. Thank goodness there's no surprise for them. But they're probably expecting to see something today, which they won't."

Liz took in a few short breaths. "But what am I going to say? That I screwed up? I can't. I'll get fired."

"You're going to have to tell Bill the truth. But offer this as an explanation to tell the client. Say the post-production house screwed up. I don't care. Tell them they had a new hire who double booked a session. When they realized the mistake, they called this morning and scheduled us for tomorrow morning."

"But Bill could get me fired."

"He could have you reprimanded, but you won't get fired. Now go. Tell him and he'll be the one to let Greg know."

Liz just sat there like a rag doll.

162

"Liz, go. I've got some work to do before I leave for the recording session."

Liz reluctantly rose from her chair. "Are you mad, Lauren?"

"I'm not too happy, but don't worry about it. At least the meeting isn't today or we'd be totally unprepared. So the client doesn't get a preview. No big deal."

"What if he doesn't like what he sees?"

"T.S., I suppose. Now out of here, please," Lauren said. She stood up and led Liz by her arm out the door and closed it behind her.

She returned to her desk and stared vacantly at the computer screen. She knew she was brusque with Liz, but she just didn't have the patience to coddle her. When Liz asked what if he--meaning Ted Bomar, the client--doesn't like what he sees, she almost laughed. That's the whole point of this presentation. He's not going to like what he sees one bit, because it's going to put him in prison. Of course, the agency will probably lose the account because of me, and I'll get fired. But if that's the price of justice, then so be it. I owe it to Michael.

Chapter 23

Returning to the bulkhead, Julio noticed a cooler, a straw tote bag, and a tackle box on the dock where the sportfisher was moored. Inside the boat were orange life vests and two fishing rods. It was obvious to Julio that the owner was preparing to go out fishing but returned to his apartment. Julio walked out on the parallel dock. Looking into the boat, he saw the key in the ignition. *Probably had to go to the bathroom*, Julio thought.

He returned to the bulkhead and sat on the low wall. He glanced at the boat and then looked into the courtyard. Having finished her laps, the woman laid on a lounge chair. Julio took a few steps toward the dock and stopped abruptly. An old man wearing white shorts and a too-tight blue knit polo shirt stretched over his pot belly came down the steps. He acknowledged Julio with a nod and stepped onto the dock. Julio did an about face and began walking south, away from the old man. That's when Julio recognized Craig behind the wheel of a large sportfisher heading toward the dock. Julio pulled the .38 Special with a silencer from his waistband and aimed the gun at Craig's head and pulled the trigger. The bullet missed Craig, but it got his attention. It took Craig a second to realize what had happened, and then he quickly turned the boat sharply to his left.

Julio took another shot at Craig and missed. He ran onto the old man's dock, leaped into the boat, and aimed the gun at the retiree who was frozen with fear.

"Get off the boat or I'll shoot!" Julio screamed. "Do it now!"

The old man put his hands up and said, "Don't shoot!" He scrambled to get out of the boat and stood on the dock staring at Julio.

Julio turned the ignition key and the engine roared. "Untie the lines! Hurry!"

The old man did as he was ordered, his hands trembling. "Push the boat away from the dock!" Julio demanded. As the boat drifted from the dock, Julio put the engine in reverse and backed up a short distance to clear the dock. He then put the gear in forward and gave it the gas. The boat thrust forward in the water, sending out a fantail. Julio saw Craig off in the distance, speeding away. Craig repeatedly glanced back to see if Julio was gaining on him. Julio followed in his wake and gave the engine more gas. People along the shoreline were screaming at them, but he couldn't hear what they were saying over the noise of the engine. Julio saw Craig turn right into a pass and overtake other boats making their way to the Gulf of Mexico. Now boaters were yelling and screaming as they were tossed in the wake of the speeding boats. Craig was through the pass and headed straight ahead. Julio followed, but the distance between the two boats grew wider. Having cleared the pass and now in the Gulf, Julio pushed the throttle up, but the boat continued to slow down. The revving of the motor was deafening. He cut back on the gas. The boat continued to drift ahead. *Hell! There must be something wrong with the propeller,* Julio thought. He looked up to see Craig's boat was far off in the distance. He saw Craig look back at him and bank the boat north. Julio slammed his hand down on the console. *Damnit! Where is he going?*

Knowing that he didn't have a chance of catching up with Craig in the Gulf, Julio turned the boat around and drifted back toward the pass. His hunch was that Craig would go back to the apartment to get his car and get the hell out of Naples. *But where? Back to Miami? Could be.*

Julio had no choice now but to dock the boat somewhere along the bay and, on foot, get to the apartment before Craig did. He certainly wasn't going back to the dock at Gulf Shore

Vista. *What if the old fart already called the police? Damn boat! Dead in the water.*

Chapter 24

Lauren picked up the phone on the first ring.

"Lauren!" Craig said out of breath.

"Craig, thank God. Where are you?"

"I'm at the apartment, but I don't have much time."

"Craig, you've got to get out of there. He knows where you are."

"I know. I just was shot at twice."

"Oh, no! Are you all right? Are you hurt? What happened?"

"I'm okay. I was out in the boat when I got your message and I was ready to call you. A scumbag was waiting for me on the dock. Shot at me. Twice. I took off for the Gulf again. He hijacked some guy's boat and chased after me. Something must have happened to the guy's propeller, though, either hit something in the water or spun the hub. I got away. I beached the boat near the condo and walked across the street. I've got to get out of here before he makes it to shore."

"Thank God you're all right. Where will you go?"

"I don't know right now. Lauren, how'd he know where to find me?"

"Judy figured it was the portable phone. He must have picked up our conversation."

"The portable phone? Damn! I've got to go. I'll try to call you."

"Craig, wait. Don't hang up. The city commissioner's meeting isn't Friday. It's tomorrow at three o'clock at City Hall. Meet me there, okay?"

"Tomorrow. Lauren, I'll try. I've got to go *now*."

The connection clicked off and Lauren hung up the receiver, closed her eyes tightly, and let out a deep sigh. The scumbag was Julio and he was in Naples! She wondered if Julio would get in touch with Sal. As far as Lauren knew, Julio and Sal knew where she lived, but not where she worked. She didn't think she was followed so she felt safe at work. But what about tonight? She didn't dare go home. What if Sal came for her?

The phone rang, startling her out of her thoughts.

"Hello."

"Hi, Lauren, it's Bill. I got the approval on the script. No changes. You did a great job.   Go ahead with your production."

"Oh, fine, thanks."

"But I must say I don't like the idea of me or the client not getting a preview of the video before the meeting tomorrow. Liz gave me the bad news."

"I know, Bill. Neither do I, but it can't be helped."

"Clients don't like surprises, Lauren."

"I know. But look. They read the script. They're familiar with the voice over talent. Presentations like this are pretty cut and dry. Trust me. It will be fine."

"All right, Lauren. I'm trusting you to do a great production job on this."

"Don't worry about it, Bill."

"Well, I do worry. This is one big client. We don't keep him happy; he'll find another agency that will. And if that happens, well, you know some people will be out of jobs."

"Bill, you worry too much."

"Yeah, that's what my wife says."

"All right. I'll see you at the meeting tomorrow."

Lauren hung up the phone before Bill could continue. She didn't know what to think anymore. Her mind was a jumble of thoughts. She was scared. She was sad. She was angry. She couldn't think clearly. She knew she had a mission to accomplish and she intended to fulfill it. She just hoped no one else got killed in the process. She looked at her watch. It was just before noon. She dialed Judy's extension and she immediately got her recording for voice mail. At the tone, Lauren left a message that she was leaving for the recording studio in North Miami and would be gone for the remainder of the day. She'd try to reach her later. Lauren put her own phone on automatic voice mail and gathered up her briefcase and purse. She took the final approved script and stopped at the photocopier and made three copies for the recording session. On the way out of the office, she stopped at Judy's office hoping she'd find her there, but the office was vacant. Lauren guessed she was in the conference room with a photographer reviewing his portfolio.

The only thing good about the long drive to the recording studio in North Miami was that it got her out of the office for a few hours, breaking up her regular routine of sitting at the computer all day. She found it amazing how much traffic there was even in non-rush hour. She always allowed herself an extra fifteen minutes in traveling time when she had an appointment because of the tremendous amount of traffic accidents that happened on every major highway in Miami-Dade County. Besides, she could always have car trouble. She thought about stopping at a fast food place and picking something up for lunch but decided to forego it. She remembered that the receptionist at the studio would take her lunch order and have the food delivered.

The recording studio was located in a warehouse district where rents were cheap and space plentiful. It was such an isolated area, Lauren always felt uneasy in the parking lot and never lingered. After she parked and locked her car, she walked briskly to the studio entrance. For security reasons, the studio kept their door locked. She pushed the doorbell and nervously waited to be allowed to enter. It was probably less than ten seconds, but to Lauren it seemed like an hour when the buzzer sounded, letting her know the door was unlocked.

Since the recording studio had to be soundproof, there was carpeting everywhere, not just the floors but the walls and ceiling, too. Lauren identified herself to Marta, the receptionist, a young coed in tight jeans and a fitted black T-shirt. Marta led Lauren down a short narrow hall to Studio A where the recording session was booked for the afternoon. She wore her dark hair in a pixie cut which emphasized her big brown eyes and high cheek bones. She opened the heavy door for Lauren and said, "Let me know if you need anything."

Lauren smiled at her. "Thank you, Marta." She turned and entered the studio. Marta closed the door behind her.

John, the owner and studio engineer, was already at his multiple-track console. Because of his dark bushy beard and plaid shirt, Lauren thought John looked more like a lumberjack than a man who produced jingles and commercials. He got up from his chair and extended his hand to greet her. He towered over her. "Hi, Lauren. Good to see you again. My condolences."

"I didn't know you knew" Lauren said, shaking his hand.

"I read the papers and I spoke to Liz in your office. Such a tragedy. How are you holding up?" He looked at Lauren, but she quickly looked away. "Make yourself comfortable."

Lauren put her briefcase and purse on the desk top and pulled out the chair. Sitting down and feeling awkward, she said, "I know I'm early and obviously the talent's not here yet. While we're waiting, do you have some stock music selections for me to hear? I don't want just a straight announce on this thing."

"Sure, but before I do that, have you had lunch?" After Lauren nodded no, John picked up the phone and called Marta. "Marta, order lunch for us, please? I'll have the meatball sub and a Coke. What about you, Lauren?"

"A kale salad with dried cranberries and roasted pecans, thank you."

"Something to drink?"

"Iced coffee, please."

John repeated Lauren's order, thanked Marta and hung up. "Okay, I've got a few good selections for you to hear. What kind of feeling are you looking for?"

"Well, this is for a developer who wants to build a Mediterranean village but needs a variance on the zoning.

The script gives a history of his projects and then makes a case for the new project. So I need something that builds for a dramatic effect."

"I have just the thing." John played several stock music selections and Lauren decided on the one John recommended. She had trusted him before on other projects and she was always pleased with the outcome.

The door opened to the studio and Marshall Taylor entered. He was a former New York TV soap opera actor who retired to South Florida. He kept his hand in the acting business by doing radio and TV commercials, plus leading roles in the local theater. Lauren thought he was quite distinguished looking, much like a doctor. In fact, when she first saw his head shot and resume, she wasn't surprised to learn that he played a doctor on "General Hospital" for many years. She liked working with Marshall because he was a true professional. He always showed up on time and could read the same script a number of different ways. Lauren thought most of the local voice-over talent mediocre who were only capable of one read. Marshall, because he was an actor, understood inflection and tone and had tremendous breath control. She could always count on him to do a first-class job.

Glancing at her watch, Lauren said, "Marshall, right on time as usual."

"I make it a point to be. How are you?"

Lauren nodded. She pulled the copies of the script from her briefcase and handed a copy to Marshall. "Here's the script. I'm sorry I wasn't able to send it to you beforehand, but I just got an approval on the copy this morning."

"That's not a problem. I'll read it over in the recording booth." Marshall turned and went into the isolation booth. There was a glass window between the two rooms so that the director and engineer could see the talent during the recording session. Lauren watched Marshall get comfortable on the high stool and put on the headphones that would allow him to hear her when she gave him direction in the reading of the script. He put the sheet of paper on the music stand and adjusted the microphone before him. Lauren reread the script just to pass the time. Meanwhile, John spliced the stock music to make it work in a ten-minute format.

After a few minutes, Marshall was ready to record. John asked him to say a few words so he could check the recording levels. Marshall said, "This is a test. This is only a test. In case of a real emergency, get the hell out of town." John laughed, but Lauren could only roll her eyes at his humor.

When the recording session was over, Marshall left the recording booth to rejoin Lauren and John who were finishing their lunch.

Lauren finished the last of her iced coffee and threw the cup in the waste basket. She took a purchase order from her file folder and filled in the blanks so that Marshall could bill the ad agency his fee. Handing the form to him, Lauren said, "Thank you, Marshall. Another great job."

"Thanks, Lauren. This Mediterranean village. It sounds really unique. It is something that's going to happen?"

"Well, the client hopes so. This script is supposed to convince the city commissioners that it's a worthwhile endeavor."

"Well, good luck to you. I'm on my way."

After Marshall left, Lauren asked John if she could use his phone while he was finishing up with the recording.

"Sure, just pick a line and dial out. I'll have you out of here in five minutes."

Lauren smiled at John and called Judy at the office. When Judy picked up the phone, Lauren said, "I'm about ready to leave the recording studio. Do you mind having some company tonight?"

Judy said, "I think that's an excellent idea."

"Good, I'll see you at your house."

Lauren hung up the phone and looked at her watch. It was a 4:45 p.m. That meant she'd be hitting the rush hour traffic. This was the time of day she dreaded. Sitting in traffic was such a waste of time.

John emailed the audio file to the video production studio with a copy going to Lauren. "You're all set, but before you go, Pete Hamlyn of Hamlyn and Cohen is looking for a creative director. Do you know of anyone I could refer him to?"

"Funny you should ask. I just might. I'll call you soon."

During the long drive to Judy's townhouse in Kendall, Lauren daydreamed that it would be perfect if she could fall into another job so easily. She figured if Ted Bomar went to prison, the agency would lose the account which meant she would be out pounding the pavement looking for work. But if she could get the creative director job, that would mean a promotion and more money. Of course, she was realistic enough to know that there was a lot of competition for a job like that. Frequently, Miami ad agencies recruited creative directors from New York agencies, thinking somehow that it would somehow add prestige to their local agency and therefore attract new clients. From what Lauren knew, new business didn't happen this way. It was more a courtship that took a long time. Frequently an agency had to woo a prospective client for a year or more. Lauren thought about opening her own ad agency, but decided she didn't have the patience to deal with clients face to face.

It was dark when Lauren arrived at Judy's place. The porch light was on and Lauren rang the bell. A soft breeze rustled the palm fronds overhead. The door opened and Judy stood there barefoot, in jeans and a teal blue Dolphins tee shirt.

Lauren looked at Judy and said, "You made good time. You already changed your clothes."

"No, not good time. I slipped out early. I was hung over all day and I'm beat."

"Right. Last night. You've got to tell me everything," Lauren said walking in. There was a soft click of the door closing. Lauren put her purse on the floor by the cocktail table and sat down on the upholstered couch.

"Can I get you something? You look a little frazzled." Judy offered.

"Yes. I'll have a Scotch and seltzer if you have it." Lauren looked around the family room. The walls displayed Judy's collection of framed prints. She focused on Gustav Klimt's "The Kiss." She admired the artist's ability of capturing the tenderness of the couple's embrace as they are enveloped by a golden robe. She thought of Michael and how tender he was with her. She missed him terribly and found it hard to believe she would never feel his kiss again.

"Lauren, here's your drink. Are you all right?" Judy asked, placing the glass on a coaster on the oak table.

Lauren sighed. "Just thinking. So tell me about last night."

Judy sat down on the club chair and sipped her drink. "Last night was a wake-up call for me."

"How so?"

"I realize I'm pretty stupid to go out on a blind date without knowing anything about the man. I mean, it would be just as stupid as if I went home with a guy I just met in a bar. When I got home last night, I sat down and prayed. I gave my thanks that nothing happened to me. I mean, dear Lord, this man, as you say, is responsible for killing Michael. He wants to have Craig killed and you, because you know the truth. If he knew that I know you, he'd probably have me killed, too. That's a damn scary thought. But you know what? It also made me very angry. Who does this man think he is? God? That he can end a person's life just because he feels like it? It's pretty sick."

"Now you understand my feelings. Michael's dead. All because of Ted Bomar. I'm going to see that he's arrested. But the guy will probably get out on bail. The guy has plenty of money. He'll hire some dream team of lawyers to defend him. I'm scared. He sent Julio to Naples to finish the job with Craig. Craig got shot at and—."

"What did you say?"

"Well, you warned me this morning about Julio. I called Craig at the condo and when I didn't get an answer, I left him a message. When I still didn't hear from him by the time I got to the office, I called him again. Finally, later this morning, Craig called to say he had to leave. That he was shot at twice when he was coming in from fishing this morning. Julio was waiting for him on the dock. Craig wasn't hurt but he's on the run. I have no idea where he is."

"Well, call him now!"

"What if...?"

"Lauren, stop it. Just call him. Does he know you're here?"

"No."

"Call him."

"All right. I have nothing to lose. He does know the city commissioner's meeting is tomorrow."

"I thought it was Friday."

"So did I. Yeah, Liz's mistake."

Lauren got up and walked into the kitchen to use the house phone. She dialed Craig's number, left a message, and she returned to the couch. Sipping her drink, she said, "I wish he'd call. Meanwhile, I want you to tell me all about last night. Did he...?"

"It was on his mind, I'm sure. But I was scared out of my mind. So I just kept drinking whatever he poured in front of me. But you know what, I didn't feel drunk. The alcohol was acting like a sedative for my jangled nerves. I knew I couldn't get off the damn boat unless I wanted to swim, so I did the only thing I could think of to put him off, and that was to be a bitch. You know, whatever the topic, I took the opposite stand. I think he was glad when we got back to the yacht club. He didn't see me home. He just sent me off with his limo driver. I don't think I'll be hearing from him again. At least, I hope not."

Lifting her glass, Lauren said, "I'll drink to that." After taking a sip, she said, "Are you sure you didn't mention anything to Bomar that would connect you and me?"

"Lauren, I'm positive. I think you should call the police."

"No. I don't think they'd arrest Ted Bomar on just what I say. They'd probably think I was crazy, especially without Craig around to back up my story. And where do I find Julio to connect him to Bomar? What I've got on Bomar has to be exposed publicly so I can be protected, and Craig, if he's still alive. I'm counting on Bomar's public reaction to what I have to say tomorrow afternoon. Then the police will take notice. They'll have to investigate."

"Will the meeting be televised?"

"The meetings are broadcast live on the public television station, but the local TV reporters always attend with video cameras in case there's something they can use on the evening news. Tune in tomorrow night on your local news station and see Bomar get what he deserves."

"Well, good luck Lauren. You're going to need it. I just hope Sal doesn't find you in the meantime."

"Me, too. Do you know what Sal looks like?

"Not really. But I can tell you about Julio. He's a Latino. Dark hair, mustache, weight lifter's body -- huge arms, thick neck. Diamond stud in one ear."

Lauren shuttered. "You mind if I stay the night? I'm afraid to go home until tomorrow night."

"Not at all, if you don't mind sleeping on the sleeper-sofa in the studio. As they say down here in glorious South Florida, *Mi case es su casa.*"

"*Gracias, senorita.*"

Chapter 25

Ted Bomar sat in his office nursing another hangover. He checked his watch to see when it was time to take his next dose of Tylenol. For the second time, he had been celebrating the death of Craig Richards. He had been at home in the media room watching the evening news with Esther when Julio called to say that he had finished the job in Naples. Mindful that Esther was listening, Ted told Julio that he didn't like to be disturbed at home, but that he forgave him this time because of the good news. Before hanging up, Ted reminded Julio that he still had some unfinished business to do. He thought that Julio sounded like he was high on something or maybe it was just the thrill of the kill. When Esther asked what was that all about, Ted responded that his foreman was bringing a project in on time.

Now that Craig was out of the way, Ted remembered to call Ray Fernandez. He dialed his secretary's extension. "Ann, get me Fernandez at Broward County Schools. Thank you."

A few minutes later, Ted's phone rang. "Hello."

"Ted, this is Ray Fernandez. How are you?"

"Good. Good. I trust you got my letter of proposal?"

"Yes, I did."

"And?"

"Well, we're looking at a few sites, yours included. We haven't reached a decision yet."

"Is there some obstacle?"

"Well, I thought we could do better on the price."

"There may room for negotiation, Ray."

"Really?"

"Yes. How much of a difference is there in price among the other properties."

"I don't know if I should disclose that."

"Well, Ray. I'm willing to be competitive on the price. What are we talking?"

Ted heard the voice end of the phone being covered at Ray's end and waited. After a moment, Ray said, "Ted, I'm going to have to call you back. I've got somebody in my office."

"Okay. I'll wait for your call." Ted sat there, worrying. He was willing to sweeten the deal personally for Ray. He wouldn't doubt it if the guy had kids in high school who were college bound. He could probably use the cash.

There was a knock at the door. "Come in."

The door opened and Ann said, "Mr. Bomar, an email from Bill Parsons just came in for you. It looks like a notice regarding the city commissioners' meeting."

"Oh, sure. I'll take it."

Ann crossed the room and handed the printout to Ted. Looking it over, he said, "It's the agenda for the meeting. The meeting starts at three, but there's other business at hand before the video presentation. Thanks, Ann."

Ann left the office as Ted continued to read Bill's email. It also listed who from the agency would be attending the meeting. He was staring at the name, but he couldn't believe what he was seeing. Ted grabbed the phone and punched in Julio's number.

Julio said, "*Que pasa?*"

Whispering, Ted said, "Julio, did you take care of the unfinished business?"

"No, man. She didn't come home last night."

"Julio, do you know where she works?"

"No."

"Why not? I thought you were going to have Sal keep an eye on her."

"I don't know, man. I don't know what Sal was doin'."

"Well, you know what, you effing idiot! She works for the effing ad agency that handles my account. It's Sindelar

Newton and Partners. They're in the Courvoisier Tower on Brickell Key. Lauren Casey will be going to the Miami City Commissioners' meeting at three o'clock today. Make sure she doesn't get there. Understand?"

"Hey, Mr. Bomar, man. I don't know what she looks like. I didn't see her going in or going out of her house."

With his anger boiling to the surface, Ted said, "Are you some kind of idiot? Do I have to tell you how to do everything? Figure it out. Check the agency's website. They might have photos of all their employees posted there. And in all probability, employees in that building have a permit number and an assigned space for parking in the garage. Persuade the attendant to give you Lauren's parking space number. Then watch the space. You'll see her. Like I said, make sure she doesn't make it to the meeting."

"Right, Mr. Bomar," Julio said. His voice had an edge that Ted picked up on. "You mind telling me where the commissioners' meeting is? Just in case?"

Ted's voice was flat. "City Hall."

"And where is City Hall?"

"On Pan American Drive in Coconut Grove. Use your app on your phone."

"Okay."

Ted hung up the phone wondering how the guy managed to tie his shoelaces in the morning.

Chapter 26

Lauren dialed Bill's office.

"This is Bill Parsons."

"Bill, it's Lauren."

"Hi. Where are you? You're not held up in the studio, are you? "

"No. I have good news. We finished early. I'm in my office. I thought I'd meet you in the conference room so I could show you the video presentation. I know you were a little upset that you weren't going to see it until the meeting at City Hall this afternoon. Do you have the time?"

"Yes, sure. I'll be right in."

"Fine. I call Greg now, too. He's going to the meeting, isn't he?"

"Well, he's trying to get out of it. He's working on a new business presentation that he's really excited about. The prospective client is paying for a creative presentation so he's working on the concepts now."

"New business, huh? That's good news. I'll see if he wants to join us, and then I'll be in a minute."

Lauren called Greg and the three convened in the conference room. They watched the video presentation silently. When it was over, Greg said, "That was a nice touch inserting that picture of Ted Bomar, the driving force behind Mirabella. That man has a huge ego so he should love seeing his face plastered on the screen. And then you give the final pitch that the Mediterranean village is a viable project. Hell, I'd vote to change the zoning."

Lauren smiled. She felt a tinge of guilt about her deception. "Thanks, Greg."

Bill looked at his watch. "The meeting's at three and it's a quarter after two now. Do you two want to drive over with me to City Hall?"

Greg spoke first. "Bill, I really want to spend the time on the new business presentation. Okay? Extend my apologies to Ted. Please?"

"Fine. I don't see any problem. And you, Lauren?"

Lauren watched Greg leave the conference room. "If you don't mind, I'd like to take my own car. City Hall is on my way home to Kendall. By the time the meeting is over, it will be late, so there's no point in coming back downtown. I figured I'd just go home from there."

"Sure. I understand. I'll see you over there." Bill started out the door and then stopped. "You'll bring the presentation?"

Lauren ejected the DVD and held it up. "I certainly will."

Lauren figured she had fifteen minutes before she needed to leave for Miami City Hall. She stopped in the ladies' room to freshen her make-up and then returned to her office. She checked her voice mail messages. There was one from her mother. Lauren made a mental note to call her this evening. She'd have a lot to tell her. There was another from Stu. He was inviting her out to dinner. Lauren groaned. Although he had been helpful that awful Sunday in the Grove, she wasn't up to socializing.

She then called Judy and immediately got connected to her voice mail again. Lauren was beginning to think Judy left her voice mail system on permanently. At the tone, Lauren said she was leaving for the meeting, to wish her luck, and that she'd call her later. She gathered up her purse, put the DVD in her briefcase and took it with her to the parking garage.

At her car, she opened her purse to get her keys. She suddenly felt uneasy and she quickly scanned the parking garage. She didn't see anyone walking around, but she felt as if someone was watching her. She quickly unlocked the door, threw her purse and briefcase on the passenger's side and got in, hitting the door locks. She started the car, fastened her seat belt, and turned on the air conditioning. Backing out of the parking space, she looked in the rearview mirror. She still didn't see anyone, but she couldn't shake the feeling there were eyes on her. She drove out of the parking garage and onto the two-lane Brickell Key Drive. When she was on the bridge that would take her back to the mainland, she checked her rearview mirror again. There was a black Corvette behind her. When she got to the traffic light on Brickell Avenue, she put on her left turn signal, heading south. The Corvette did the same. Brickell Avenue was a four-lane road with a landscaped median strip dividing the avenue into north and southbound traffic. Lauren stayed in the right hand lane. The Corvette followed her. In front of her, a Mercedes slowed down to make a right turn and rather than brake, Lauren drove into the left lane in front of a white van. She checked her rearview mirror and she no longer saw the Corvette. She wondered if the driver had turned off as well. She hoped so.

Traffic was moving smoothly along Brickell, past the high-rise condominiums. Several of the buildings were very unique architecturally and were showcased in *Architectural Digest* when they first opened. Her personal favorite was the building that looked like a giant cruise ship.

As she approached the intersection of Brickell Avenue and South Bayshore Drive, Lauren put on her left signal and turned into the left turn lane. Braking to a stop behind another car, she glanced in her rearview mirror. Damn! Right behind her was the black Corvette. With its sleek aerodynamic design, the car looked like a shark. She looked ahead. The left turn traffic signal turned green and Lauren followed the cars to South Bayshore Drive, one of the main roads into the heart of Coconut Grove. This was another four-lane road which narrowed to two lanes. Lauren stayed in the left lane. She drove past Viscaya, an Italianate villa built by James Deering in the 1910s and the Science Museum and Planetarium. She passed a walled-in residential community and Mercy Hospital which fronted Biscayne Bay. She glanced in her rearview mirror and again saw that the Corvette was tailing her. The driver now swerved into the right hand lane, speeding up. Lauren thought, Oh, another jerk trying to pass on the right.

Suddenly, the glass on the passenger side shattered raining crystal shards everywhere. She looked to her right and saw a gun aimed at her. Lauren instinctively ducked and jammed her foot on the accelerator, speeding ahead of the Corvette. Another shot, missing her, but shattering her backseat window. Again more glass littered the car's interior. She swerved in front of the Corvette into the right lane. In no time she was on the bumper of a car obeying the forty-mile per hour speed limit. She quickly passed the car on the left and swerved back into the right lane. Just ahead on the right, she saw a side street. She slowed down enough to maneuver the turn and then accelerated to Tigertail Avenue which ran parallel to South Bayshore Drive. She was panic-stricken and gripped the steering wheel tightly, her knuckles turning white. She turned left onto Tigertail and sped down the quiet, two-lane residential street. Again, she looked for the Corvette and saw that it was gaining on her. She had to get away but where could she go? She saw the Corvette pull out of the right lane to pass her on the left. She thought he was probably going to take another shot at her or cut her off. Not waiting to find out, she slammed on her brakes. As she expected, the driver fired at her as he whizzed by. She made a U-turn and hit the gas, hoping she could lose him down one of the side streets. She heard the Vet's brakes screech. At the next side street, she slowed, turned left, drove to the end of the street and turned right. Two houses down on her right, she saw an eight-foot wooden privacy fence that completely blocked Lauren's vision of the house. Just before the neighboring house, there was a paved driveway with the gate open. Lauren slammed her foot on her brake and drove in past the gate and veered right onto the manicured lawn. She knew she was trespassing and she didn't care if the owners came out. Her car was hidden from view. She got out of her car, sending glass shards from her lap to the grass. She ran for the gate and pushed it closed. The roar of the Vet's engine sent Lauren running back to her car, praying that the driver didn't see her. Her heart pounding in her ears, she knew she was trapped. She listened for the Vet to slow down or stop. The sound of the engine diminished as the Corvette continued down the street until finally there was silence. All she heard were the chirping of the birds and the palm fronds rustling in the wind. She heard the crunching of leaves and turned to look. It was a squirrel running toward a Schefflera tree. It scampered up the trunk and ran along the branches, shaking a large leaf loose. Lauren looked at the house. It was immense, very modern with floor-to-ceiling windows in a pale grey stucco finish with a Mediterranean barrel tile roof. She walked along the brick pathway to the front door and rang the doorbell. She didn't know what she would say to the owner, but she was scared and her hands trembled. There was no response. She pushed the doorbell again. She waited for a voice announcing, "I'm coming," but there was only silence. Lauren walked back to her car and waited. She checked the time. It was already three o'clock. The meeting at City Hall had just begun. Then she heard the familiar rumble of the Vet's engine, only this time she could hear that the car was driving slowly down the street. Lauren held her breath and prayed, please, dear God, don't let him stop. Make him keep going. The sound of the engine became more distant until there was silence again.

Lauren debated if she should leave or stay. She had to get to the meeting. She wondered if the driver of the Vet knew her destination, and if he would be lying in wait. Or was he still searching the little side streets of Coconut Grove? She heard another car coming. Then engine purred in contrast to the roar of the Vet. It, too, traveled past the fenced-in house. After twenty minutes, Lauren got up her courage to leave her temporary fortress. She got in her car and backed it around so she could drive out facing forward. She put the car in park, got out and slowly opened the gate. She looked up and down the street for the black Corvette. There wasn't a car in sight on the quiet, banyan tree-lined street. She ran back to her car, got in, and drove off, heading back to Tigertail Avenue. She kept checking her rearview mirror and looked down side streets, hoping she would not see her would-be assassin.

At Twenty-Seventh Avenue, the next intersection, she made a left and drove the short block to South Bayshore Drive. At the traffic signal, she checked her watch. She was just minutes away, and she hoped there was still time to make the presentation. She knew that by going to City Hall, she was taking a chance of getting killed. She thought back to the parking garage. The driver of the Vet had to have followed her from there. And unless Sal had a mustache, too, it had to be Julio. And how did he find out where I worked? She had to get inside City Hall before Julio arrived.

Finally she saw the sign for Miami City Hall. As she turned left onto the drive that would lead her there, Lauren said a silent prayer that Julio wasn't waiting for her. The building was up on the left, an old Art Deco building. Lauren searched for a place to park, all the while keeping her eyes open for the black Vet.

When Lauren finally parked, she took her briefcase and purse and ran to the entrance to City Hall. She flew into the auditorium and all eyes turned to her.

"Excuse me, I'm sorry I'm late," said Lauren, gulping for air. She walked down the center aisle to the front of the room. There were more people in attendance than she had expected, and local television station video cameras were set up around the room.

Facing the audience on the dais sat the six commissioners, the mayor, and the city manager in high-back leather chairs. There were microphones in front of each. The one in the middle, an elderly Latin male, said, "Are you the young lady with the video presentation?"

"Yes, I am, sir."

"Good, then." The commissioner gestured to Lauren's left. "Since you weren't here, Mr. Bomar was just about to proceed without you and give us a presentation regarding a zoning variance to allow for his Mediterranean village. Now that you are here, we might as well stick to the plan."

The Deadly Game

Lauren glanced to her left. A stocky, middle-aged man with blond hair wearing an expensive tailored suit looked shocked to see her and then quickly composed himself. So this was Ted Bomar! He took the first seat in the first row.

"I'll just be a sec." Lauren put her purse and briefcase down on an empty seat in the first row. She opened the briefcase, got out the DVD, and laptop computer. She hooked up the cable to the monitor, inserted the disk with trembling hands, and picked up the remote. She felt a tap on her shoulder and she jerked, turning to see who it was. "Oh, Bill. You startled me."

Bill put up his hands. "Sorry, Lauren. Where were you? Did you have car trouble? You know you should keep a cell phone with you."

Lauren looked up at his eyes and nodded. "It's a long story. I'll tell you when this is over."

Lauren watched Bill take his seat next to Ted and then looked around the room. She started the video and credits rolled. The instruction featured an animated Mirabella logo with dramatic music.

Over pictures of architectural details, lifestyle interiors, couples at poolside, Marshall Taylor's prerecorded narration began: "Environmental preservation. Architectural excellence. Elegant lifestyles. These are the key factors that distinguish a Mirabella development. And their approach to land development has served them well. They have enjoyed a successful track record for over 30 years with residential and commercial projects throughout the state of Florida."

The video presentation continued with reference to specific properties, how fast they sold out and how many families were living in Mirabella communities. Lauren looked at the faces in the room. Their attention was on the monitors, some even nodded their heads recognizing the projects.

The video presentation continued. "And now on the drawing board comes a new concept for Miami, but one that is not really new at all. It is a synthesis of an age-old ideal. A Mediterranean village that offers a European mode of living--quaint shops, outdoor cafes, waterfront restaurants, a marina, a yacht club, and charming residences--all with the ambiance of a seaside resort along the French Riviera. An extraordinary place, Mediterranean village is the concept of Ted Bomar, the driving force behind Mirabella."

Now the audience was focusing on the picture of Ted Bomar. They would never see the rest of the video presentation that Lauren had produced. She froze the video by pressing the pause button and cut off the sound with the mute button.

Lauren picked up the microphone from the podium. In a clear, even voice, she began, "Yes, Ted Bomar, the driving force behind Mirabella. And a force to be reckoned with. Because, you see, Ted Bomar is a murderer. He murdered my husband, Michael Casey."

Ted shot up out of his seat. "Who are you? Are you out of your mind? I don't even know your husband. What you're saying is absurd!"

Everyone in the audience was talking at once.

Lauren shouted. "Hear me out. What I am telling you is the truth."

The audience fell silent.

"You see, ladies and gentlemen, Ted Bomar is a very tyrant who always gets his way. He's made fortunes in land deals, always making huge profits. Well, this time he has a piece of property which he is negotiating to sell to Broward County Schools. The asking price is somewhere in the three to four million dollar range. On the surface, that's fine. But when we dig a little deeper, do our research if you will, we find out that this property is a toxic site. It's not safe for building anything on it, let alone a school. Someday, maybe, after a massive clean-up, but that would cost millions of dollars to make it environmentally safe. Mr. Bomar had no intention of revealing there was anything wrong with the property. In fact, he planned to bribe whoever he had to in order to sell the land. And that's where he ran into trouble. Mr. Bomar didn't count on having Craig Richards trying to stop him. Craig Richards is Mr. Bomar's or perhaps I should say *was* Mr. Bomar's vice president of marketing. Craig Richards is now missing."

Lauren saw the audience shifting their eyes from her to Bomar and back again. "One night after too many drinks, Mr. Bomar bragged to Craig Richards about the property he planned to unload on the school district. Mr. Richards told Mr. Bomar he couldn't get away with it. That he wouldn't allow it to happen. Mr. Bomar believed there was only one way to deal with Mr. Richards. And that was to get rid of him. He hired a gunman, Julio, who stalked Mr. Richards until he knew his routine. The assassin planned his hit on a Sunday afternoon when Mr. Richards went for his usual bike ride through Coconut Grove. Unfortunately, for my husband, Michael Casey, Craig Richards was ill that day and stayed home. Julio had no way of knowing this, but my husband is a dead ringer for Craig Richards so he was shot and killed instead. You may have seen the story in the newspapers." Lauren held up the newspaper page with Michael's photo. "This is my husband." She held up a photo of Craig Richards. "This is Craig Richards."

The video cameras zoomed in for a tight shot. The audience buzzed like a nest of bees.

Lauren turned to face Ted Bomar who was red in the face, his eyes bulging with anger. "You see, Mr. Bomar, You had a motive and I have proof."

Lauren held up the file folder she had stolen from Ted Bomar's office.

"Where did you get that?" Ted demanded.

"Your office. It's the file that contains the proposal to the Broward County School district."

"It will never stand up in court. You didn't get that with a search warrant."

"Mr. Bomar, I'm not the police. I'm a widow. And I am going to see that you go to prison. Ted shot out of his seat and yelled. "I didn't kill your husband."

"You certainly did. You hired someone to do it for you."

"That's a lie! I'm not going to stand for this. How dare you! You're crazy. I'm out of here!"

Ted turned and headed down the center aisle, pushing Lauren out of his way. Lauren lost her balance and fell back, landing on her rear end. She struggled to stand up and turned her head to see Ted stop in the middle of his stride. He said, "And where have you been? A fine job you did! You dumb imbecile!

There was a popping sound and Ted fell back clutching his chest. Lauren looked to see a Julio poised with a .38 Special. He aimed and shot again, this time shooting Ted Bomar in the forehead. Everyone in the audience screamed. Some people hit the floor, scrambling on hands and knees to vacate the auditorium. Others just ran out the door, trying to escape, even if it meant getting shot. An off-duty police officer ran up behind the gunman, drew his service revolver and yelled, "Freeze. Police. Drop the gun or I'll shoot."

Julio hesitated and dropped the gun at his feet. The police officer stepped around the man and kicked the gun out of reach. "On the floor, hands behind your back, and spread 'em."

After a few moments, Lauren could hear police sirens getting louder and louder as they approached City Hall. She looked at Ted Bomar. His eyes were open, but they saw nothing. Blood soaked his fine shirt, tie and suit. The carpet under his head was turning crimson. She looked up and saw Julio being led away, handcuffed. She felt a tap on her shoulder and turned. "Lauren, are you all right?" It was Craig Richards. Lauren fell into his arms and said, "Craig, I thought you were dead. Oh, God, did you see him? He's dead. He's dead."

Lauren was trembling and began to sob, softly at first and then uncontrollably. He held her tight, rocking her gently like one would a child who had a nightmare. He murmured in her ear, "It's over, Lauren. Justice has been done. And you know something? It's all over now. We're going to be all right."

The Deadly Game

ACKNOWLEDGEMENTS

Thank you, dear reader, for spending your leisure time reading **The Deadly Game.** I hope you enjoyed it.

To my husband Barry, for his support and feedback while I was developing the plot. And for his critical eye while creating a book cover. To my daughter Valerie for encouraging me every step of the way. And to my cousin Judy Johnson for her love and interest in everything I do.

Thank you to my friend and author Ang Pompano who urged me to publish this book and volunteered his time and knowledge to help me succeed. Thank you Mark Dressler, also a friend and author who provided insights and support.

Special recognition goes to Hugh Williams of Just2Creative for assisting me in finishing my cover design. He's an exceptional graphic designer and artist.

I recognize Rita Cohl. The arrangement we made, exchanging chapters each week of our work in progress motivated me to put this story down on paper. I was grateful to have your suggestions and your friendship.

My gratitude goes to Tom Savage, a fellow MWA member and best-selling author who I was fortunate to have as a mentor on this novel. His praise for my plot, characters and setting plus wise suggestions enabled me to edit the manuscript with an eye to making every word count.

A special acknowledgement to Ray Allen, the best mentor a copywriter could ever hope to have. He was instrumental in shaping my career. His advertising agency, Caravetta Allen Kimbrough was the best place to work in Miami.

I'm thankful for a long and successful career in advertising that provided me enough fodder for many more novels. The clients, co-workers and vendors that I enjoyed working with are too numerous to list here.

I would be remiss not to mention the librarians at Broward County Library system for assistance in researching the EPA Super Fund sites in Florida.

Of course I must thank all my dear friends who were persistent in asking me when this novel will be published. Sharon Allison, Janice Jacobs, Judy Kaplan and Rita in South Florida. In Connecticut: Nancy McCormick, and Joan Merton. It's finally here. I hope you enjoy the read.

AUTHOR'S NOTE

The kernel of the idea for this novel came from personal experience. My husband and I had a habit of going for Sunday bike rides through Coconut Grove, Matheson Hammock and Old Cutler Road. As described in the opening pages of this book, he did play his game of racing ahead, hiding and then scaring me when he came from behind and tapped me on the shoulder. As many writers do, I said to myself, what if he disappeared? Then what?

One thing led to another in outlining a plot, but I needed a motive for a murder and a villain. What better than greed and a Florida real estate developer?

Building a school on top of a toxic site is not new. Research reveals many schools across the country sit on land where toxic chemicals and other industrial waste had been dumped or buried. Children, teachers and staff may suffer severe health problems, including learning disabilities from contaminated soil, gases and water. Once discovered, contact should be made to one of the 10 EPA regional offices.

Toxic waste dumps came to national attention in the late 70s when Love Canal and Valley of the Drums were proven to pose a detrimental risk to health and the environment.

In response, Congress enacted in 1980 the Comprehensive Environmental Response, Compensation and Reliability Act, informally called Superfund. It allows the EPA to force responsible parties to either perform cleanups or reimburse the government for the work. When there is no viable party, the Superfund gives the EPA the funds and the authority to clean up contaminated sites.

To learn more about Superfund, visit www.epa.gov/superfund. You may search for Superfund sites where you live.

The Deadly Game

ABOUT THE AUTHOR

A native of New Jersey, Lynn Sheft earned her bachelor's degree from the University of Miami and established herself as a professional copywriter and creative director in South Florida. During her career, she won numerous awards for her campaigns for regional and national consumer accounts. In addition, she wrote articles for magazines, provided editing services and was an adjunct instructor teaching ESL classes.

When she relocated to Connecticut, she turned to writing fiction full time, including short stories and novels. THE DEADLY GAME is her debut novel. Visit her website www.lynnsheft.com for news about further publications.

She is a member of Mystery Writers of America and lives in Madison, Connecticut with her husband Barry.

Credit: Kiernan Photography

The Deadly Game

Made in United States
Orlando, FL
20 December 2021

12279758R00125